LOÏC NICOLOFF - ANTOINE LOSTY - ALBERTO ZANON - ROBERTA PIERPAOLI

THE GREEN GIRLS

Graphic Universe™ • Minneapolis

ABOUT THE CREATORS

LOÏC NICOLOFF

Loïc Nicoloff writes scripts for films, TV, and comics. After having directed nearly twenty short films, most of which have won awards in France and abroad, he is preparing his first feature film. Whether his stories take place in the contemporary world or in fantasy worlds, he wants to create bubbles of imagination—places where readers can escape and live out extraordinary adventures.

ANTOINE LOSTY

After three years in an animation school in Bordeaux, French comic book illustrator and designer Antoine Losty released his comic *Splash* through Dupuis in 2020. He is particularly fond of working with light and color in his illustrations. He is active on—and draws inspiration from—Instagram.

ALBERTO ZANON

Alberto Zanon is an illustrator based in Italy. He graduated from the Scuola del Fumetto di Milano and the Disney Academy Milano. In addition to his work on graphic novels, he has been a character designer and concept artist since 1998.

ROBERTA PIERPAOLI

Roberta Pierpaoli has worked as a background artist for cartoons and illustrated several books for the Italian publishers Piemme Edizioni, Cronaca di Topolina, and Tatai Lab. She has also contributed to graphic novels for French publishers such as Soleil and Jungle.

ABOUT THE TRANSLATOR

PERCY LEED

Percy Leed writes nonfiction books for children, covering topics from sports to science. He lives in Minneapolis, Minnesota. *The Green Girls* is his first graphic novel translation.

Les belles vertes volume 1, *Sauvons les océans!*, copyright © 2020 by Jungle
Written by Loïc Nicoloff and illustrated by Alberto Zanon and Antoine Losty

Les belles vertes volume 2, *Sauvons les orangs-outans!*, copyright © 2021 by Jungle
Written by Loïc Nicoloff and illustrated by Roberta Pierpaoli and Antoine Losty

Translated from the French by Percy Leed
English-language translation copyright © 2022 by Lerner Publishing Group, Inc.

Graphic Universe™ is a trademark of Lerner Publishing Group, Inc.

Graphic Universe™
An imprint of Lerner Publishing Group, Inc.
241 First Avenue North
Minneapolis, MN 55401 USA

For reading levels and more information, look up this title at www.lernerbooks.com.

Main body text set in Dinkle.
Typeface provided by Chank.

Library of Congress Cataloging-in-Publication Data

Names: Nicoloff, Loïc, writer. | Losty, Antoine, illustrator. | Zanon, Alberto, illustrator. | Pierpaoli, Roberta, illustrator. | Leed, Percy, 1968– translator.
Title: The green girls / Loïc Nicoloff, Antoine Losty, Alberto Zanon, Roberta Pierpaoli ; translation by Percy Leed.
Other titles: Belles vertes. English
Description: Minneapolis : Graphic Universe, [2023] | Les belles vertes volume 1, Sauvons les océans!, copyright ©2020 by Jungle ; Written by Loïc Nicoloff and illustrated by Alberto Zanon and Antoine Losty — Les belles vertes volume 2, Sauvons les orangs-outans!, copyright ©2021 by Jungle ; Written by Loïc Nicoloff and illustrated by Roberta Pierpaoli and Antoine Losty | Audience: Ages 9–14 | Audience: Grades 7–9 | Summary: "Emma, Lily, and Fadila want to save the planet . . . and no one around them seems to care. Frustrated, they call themselves the Green Girls, take to social media, and launch a series of bold protests." —Provided by publisher.
Identifiers: LCCN 2022019429 (print) | LCCN 2022019430 (ebook) | ISBN 9781728460369 (library binding) | ISBN 9781728478227 (paperback) | ISBN 9781728480497 (ebook)
Subjects: CYAC: Graphic novels. | Protest movements—Fiction. | Environmental protection—Fiction. | LCGFT: Ecofiction. | Graphic novels.
Classification: LCC PZ7.7.N536 Gr 2023 (print) | LCC PZ7.7.N536 (ebook) | DDC 741.5/944—dc23/eng/20220426

LC record available at https://lccn.loc.gov/2022019429
LC ebook record available at https://lccn.loc.gov/2022019430

Manufactured in the United States of America
2-1009740-50376-6/2/2023

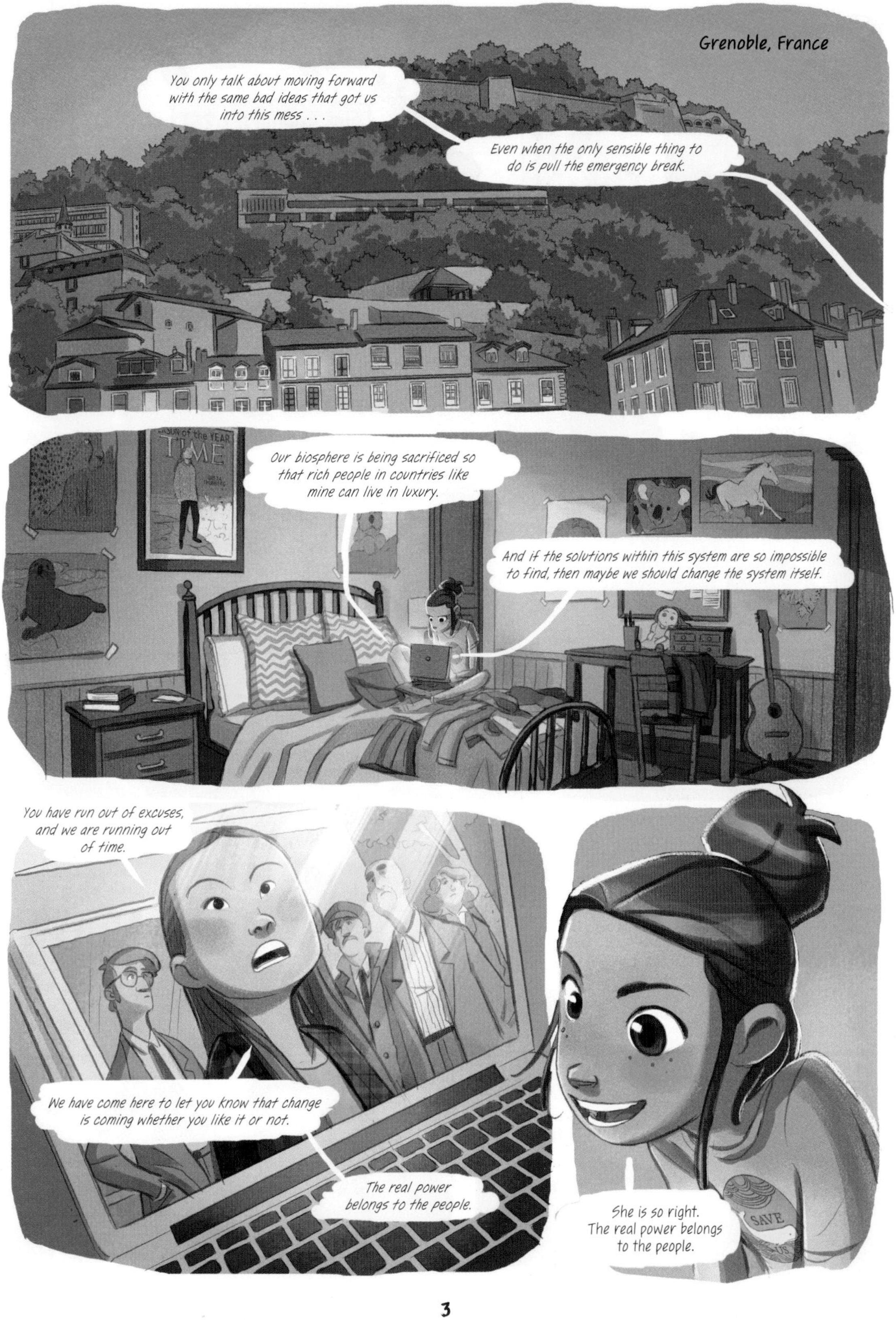
Grenoble, France
You only talk about moving forward with the same bad ideas that got us into this mess . . .
Even when the only sensible thing to do is pull the emergency break.
Our biosphere is being sacrificed so that rich people in countries like mine can live in luxury.
And if the solutions within this system are so impossible to find, then maybe we should change the system itself.
You have run out of excuses, and we are running out of time.
We have come here to let you know that change is coming whether you like it or not.
The real power belongs to the people.
She is so right. The real power belongs to the people.

The real power belongs to the people!

That's why, right here, we're going to create . . .

An organic vegetable garden!

Ta-daaaa!

OUR SCHOOL'S FIRST ORGANIC GARDEN

A square of land where everyone can plant whatever vegetable they want.

With peasant seeds, of course.

And with no chemical fertilizers!

This way, we'll learn more about farm work, natural cycles . . .

And what ends up on our plates.

What a great idea!

Now does anyone have questions?

A vegetable garden? Really?

Do we look like a bunch of peasants? No thanks!

HA HA HA HA

peasant seed: all or part of a plant organ meant for reproduction, selected by a farmer working with a population of the plant. The use of peasant seeds is part of an agricultural movement in France.

Uhhhhh . . .

Young lady, please ask a real question or we'll give the floor to someone else!

I *am* being real! What's the point of growing our own vegetables?

We can get them year-round at the grocery!

Yeah, plus . . .

Then we don't get our hands dirty!

Exactly. It's not natural to get tomatoes in winter.

They're full of pesticides . . .

And grown in huge greenhouses!

Chill out, you three. You're all turning red . . .

Like a bunch of tomatoes!

And not even organic.

HA HA HA HA

Emma, Lily, and Fadila . . .

The Tomato-Heads!

Don't listen, Emma!

They're wrong!

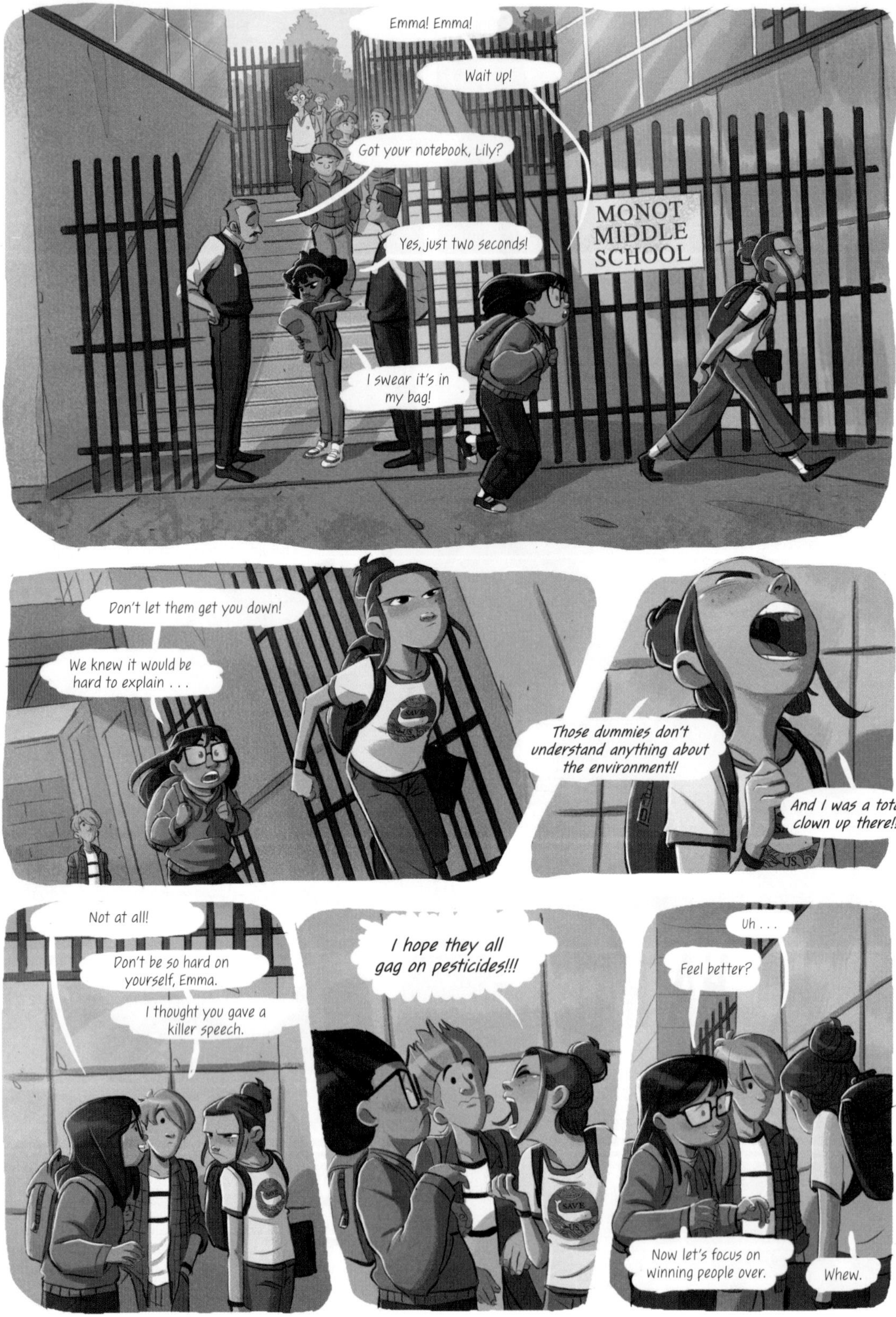

Emma! Emma!
Wait up!
Got your notebook, Lily?
MONOT MIDDLE SCHOOL
Yes, just two seconds!
I swear it's in my bag!
Don't let them get you down!
We knew it would be hard to explain . . .
Those dummies don't understand anything about the environment!!
And I was a total clown up there!!!
Not at all!
Don't be so hard on yourself, Emma.
I thought you gave a killer speech.
I hope they all gag on pesticides!!!
Uh . . .
Feel better?
Now let's focus on winning people over.
Whew.

I'm so tired of people *not caring*.

It's meee!

So how did it go?

Emma, you forgot to take out the trash earlier . . .

And it's your turn to do the dishes.

Pssh! Fine, I hear you . . .

I'll get around to it!

Wasn't today her big presentation?

Today? I can't remember . . .

BLAM!!!!

They don't get it . . .

Being thirteen sucks!

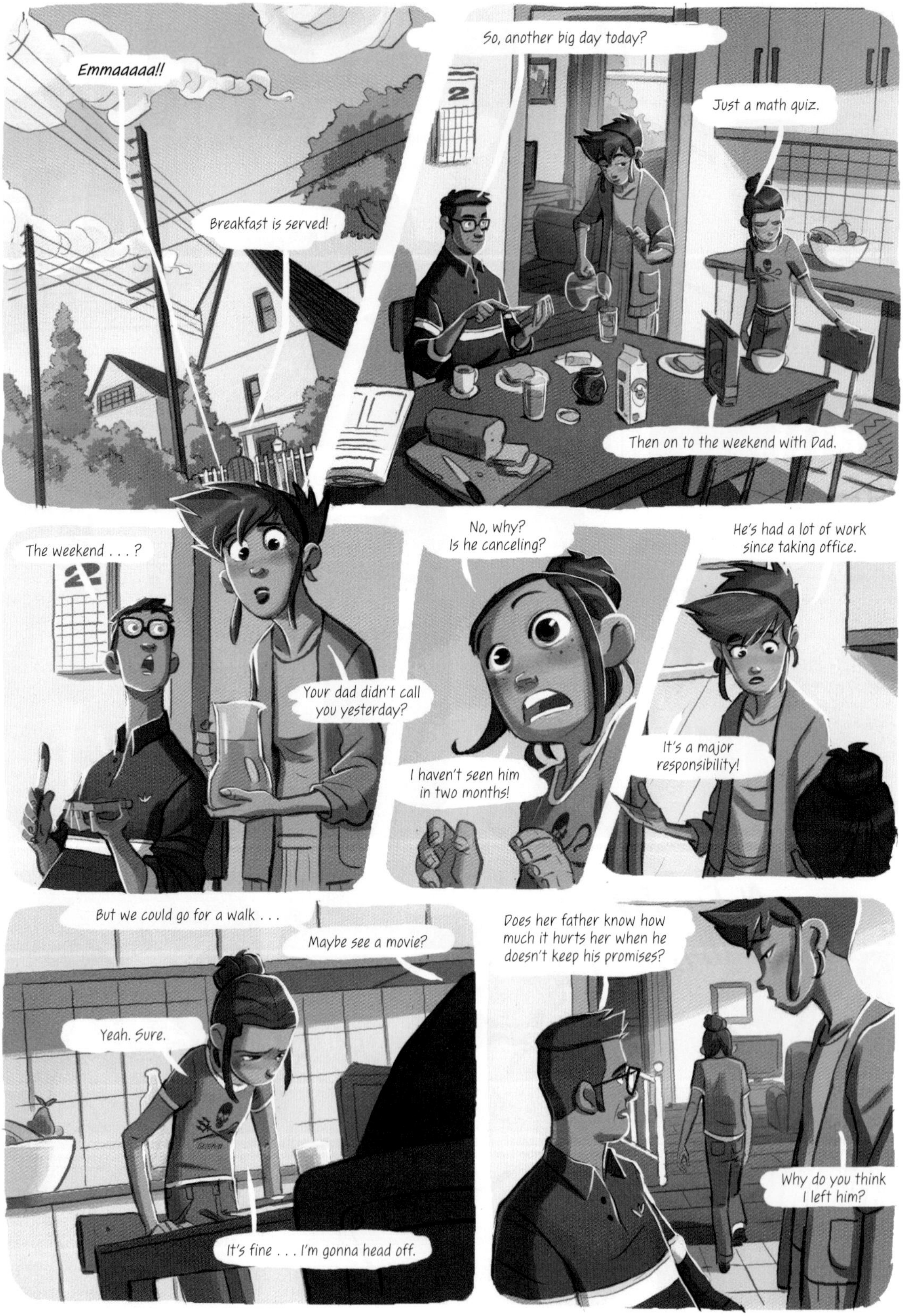

Emmaaaaa!!
Breakfast is served!
So, another big day today?
Just a math quiz.
Then on to the weekend with Dad.
The weekend . . . ?
Your dad didn't call you yesterday?
No, why? Is he canceling?
I haven't seen him in two months!
He's had a lot of work since taking office.
It's a major responsibility!
But we could go for a walk . . .
Maybe see a movie?
Yeah. Sure.
It's fine . . . I'm gonna head off.
Does her father know how much it hurts her when he doesn't keep his promises?
Why do you think I left him?

I am *so. Fed. Up!*

It's been two months since I saw him. Two months!

I hate him!

Uhh, hi Emma. You look like you just reached your limit.

You lose your *Fortnite* password or what?

My dad canceled again . . .

And what is that monstrosity!?

???

Allow me to present Lady Mim.

She's a domesticated shrew.

Isn't she cute? Now we go everywhere together!

Until she escapes. Like your ferret.

Or you forget about it, like your guinea pig!

C'mon! You two suck!

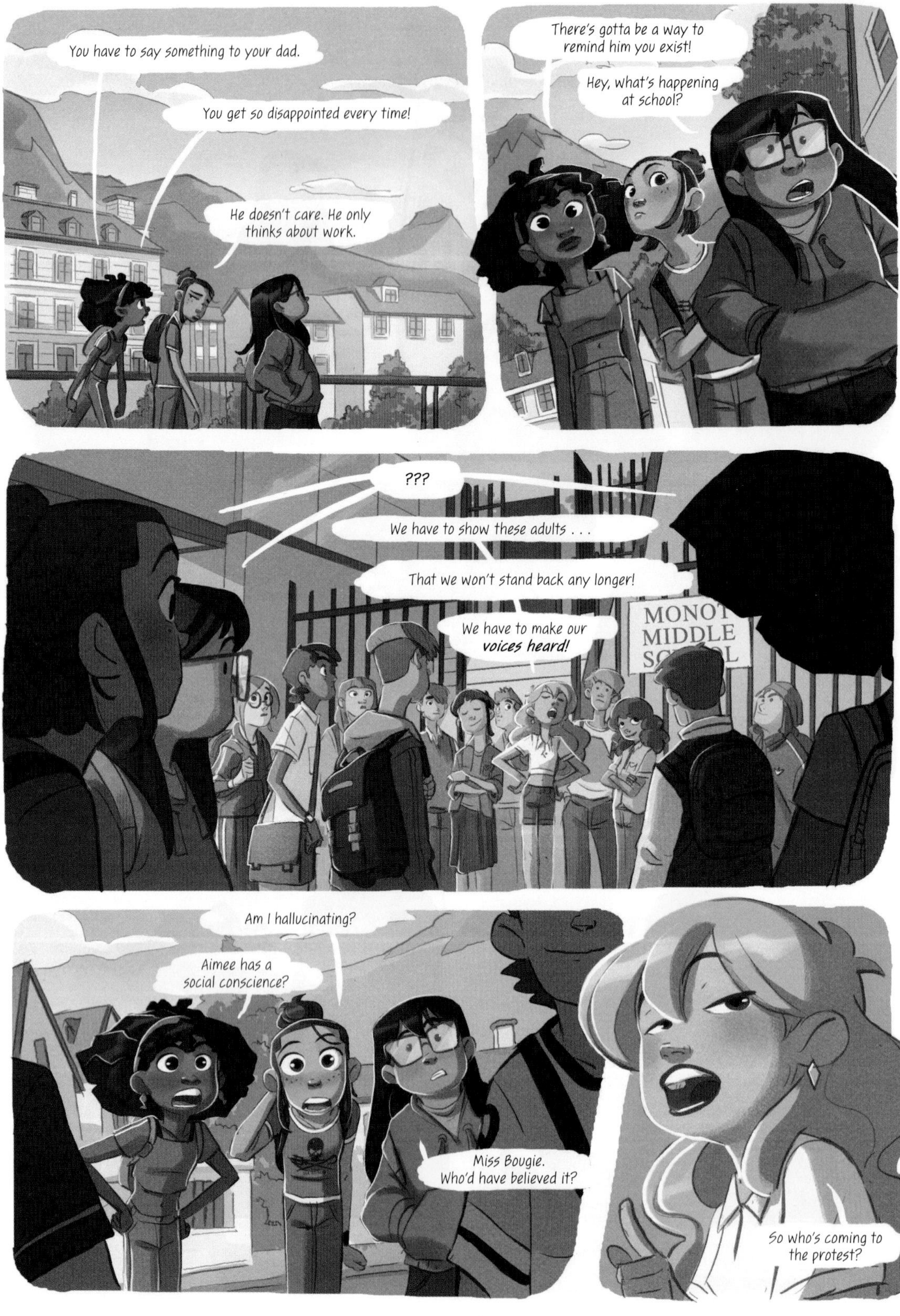
You have to say something to your dad.
You get so disappointed every time!
He doesn't care. He only thinks about work.
There's gotta be a way to remind him you exist!
Hey, what's happening at school?
???
We have to show these adults . . .
That we won't stand back any longer!
We have to make our *voices heard!*
MONOT MIDDLE SCHOOL
Am I hallucinating?
Aimee has a social conscience?
Miss Bougie. Who'd have believed it?
So who's coming to the protest?

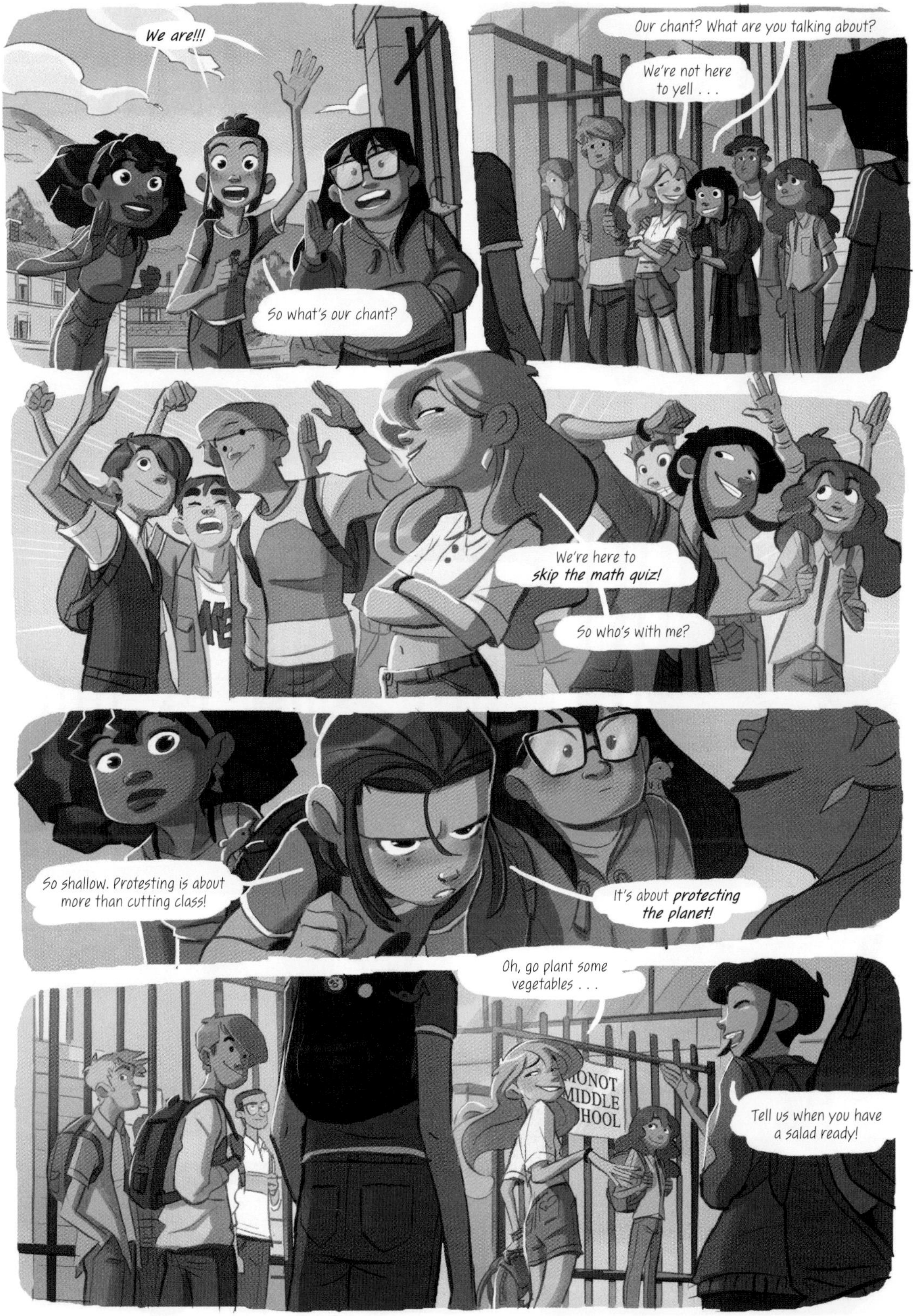
We are!!!
So what's our chant?
Our chant? What are you talking about?
We're not here to yell . . .
We're here to skip the math quiz!
So who's with me?
So shallow. Protesting is about more than cutting class!
It's about protecting the planet!
Oh, go plant some vegetables . . .
MONOT MIDDLE SCHOOL
Tell us when you have a salad ready!

Uh, guys?

Is it just me, or is everyone shallow at this school?

COLLEGE PHILIPPE MONOT

It *is* pretty messed up.

But not surprising.

So that's it?

A youth protest . . .

As an excuse to skip class?

It's a start.

There's a long way to go!

If every student, in every country, really took to the streets . . .

Just imagine the *panic*.

Alert! Alert! Young people on the loose!

Run! Go home!

They've gone green!

Ha ha ha ha!

Look out! Red alert!

Hey, why aren't you at the protest?

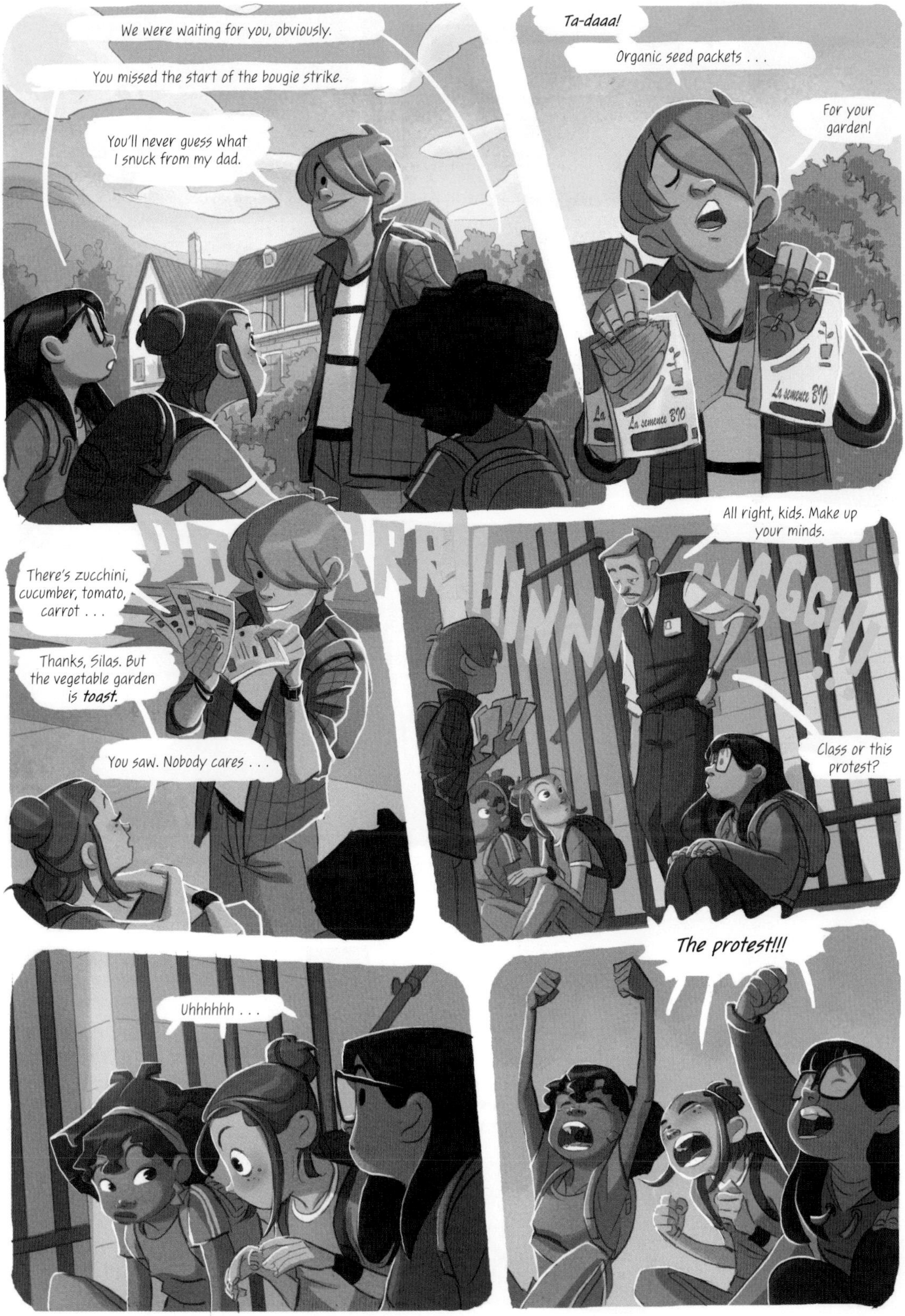
We were waiting for you, obviously.
You missed the start of the bougie strike.
You'll never guess what I snuck from my dad.
Ta-daaa!
Organic seed packets . . .
For your garden!
La semence BIO
La semence BIO
There's zucchini, cucumber, tomato, carrot . . .
Thanks, Silas. But the vegetable garden is *toast.*
You saw. Nobody cares . . .
All right, kids. Make up your minds.
Class or this protest?
Uhhhhhh . . .
The protest!!!

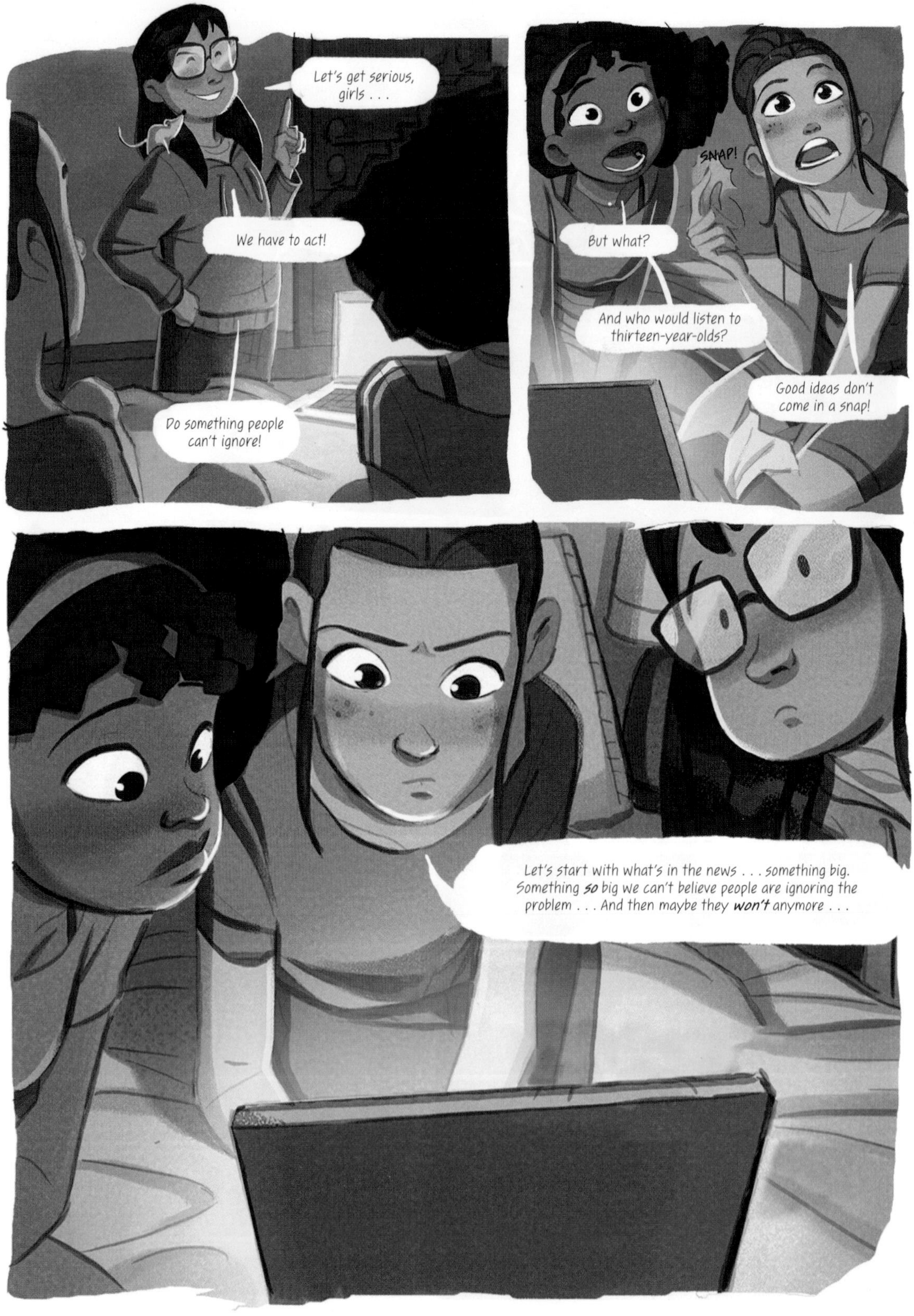
Let's get serious, girls . . .
We have to act!
Do something people can't ignore!
But what?
SNAP!
And who would listen to thirteen-year-olds?
Good ideas don't come in a snap!
Let's start with what's in the news . . . something big. Something *so* big we can't believe people are ignoring the problem . . . And then maybe they ***won't*** anymore . . .

That's it!

The Argo!

Huh? What's that?

No, no!

The Argo is the biggest container ship in the world!

22,000 containers! Four football fields long!

It's huge!

It launches in three days from Saint-Nazaire.

That's our time to act!

Yeah, right! We just steal your parents' car and dart over.

And leave the ship a little parting gift . . .

You mean the movie?

Booooooom!

Pow!

Pssh! Not **exactly** what I meant.

Just saying: problem solved.

Yep, then we're good. It'll only be huge cruise ships polluting.

I'm serious!

I'll show you.

CONTAINER CARRIERS, SCOURGE OF THE SEAS

More than 50,000 ships, on seas across the globe, transport nearly 45 million containers, or more than 90 percent of the world's goods. But are they the key to a booming business or a bust for the environment?

Polluting the sea . . . and the air

For years, people have raised their voices against pollution from ocean liners, floating luxury hotels that consume between 60 and 150 tons of heavy fuel oil per day. But the record of container ships is no better, as they also consume heavy fuel oil.

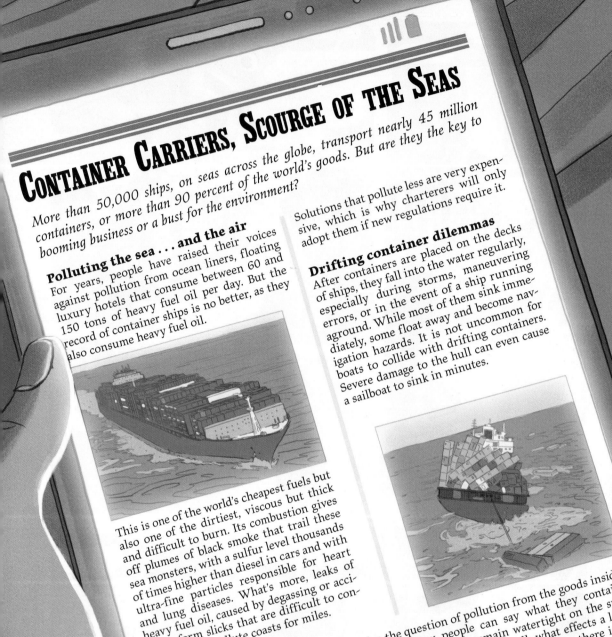

This is one of the world's cheapest fuels but also one of the dirtiest, viscous but thick and difficult to burn. Its combustion gives off plumes of black smoke that trail these sea monsters, with a sulfur level thousands of times higher than diesel in cars and with ultra-fine particles responsible for heart and lung diseases. What's more, leaks of heavy fuel oil, caused by degassing or accidents, form slicks that are difficult to contain and can pollute coasts for miles.

Solutions that pollute less are very expensive, which is why charterers will only adopt them if new regulations require it.

Drifting container dilemmas

After containers are placed on the decks of ships, they fall into the water regularly, especially during storms, maneuvering errors, or in the event of a ship running aground. While most of them sink immediately, some float away and become navigation hazards. It is not uncommon for boats to collide with drifting containers. Severe damage to the hull can even cause a sailboat to sink in minutes.

There is also the question of pollution from the goods inside these containers. Few people can say what they contain, whether the containers will remain watertight on the surface or in shallow waters, and above all, what effects a long period in salt water has on containers. To date, there is no guaranteed way to locate lost containers, and no progr

Toward a commercial revolution

To save the planet and the oceans, environmental groups are campaigning for increases in the cost of fuel oil and limitations on container ship traffic—for less pollution, fewer container losses at sea, and fewer collisions.

Economists see potential results that would change the face of trade: if the cost of transportation increased, Western manufacturers would be interested in bringing production sites closer to their consumers, creating local jobs and boosting local economies.

The giant monsters of a global economy

For decades, production of many everyday consumer products has shifted from Western nations to Asian nations for two main reasons.

One is a cheaper labor force due to looser regulations on wages, the number of working hours per day and per week, and sometimes on the starting age of workers.

Another is that the transportation of these goods is very cheap, even if it is slow, for one essential reason: heavy fuel oil is a low-cost, little-taxed fuel. This is due to international agreements that, from the 1970s onward, have been almost impossible to change.

Powerful charterers are therefore building larger and larger freighters, making the use of their ships profitable by loading more and more containers.

Their latest feat: the Argo, a sea monster that will be able to carry 22,000 containers, and which will launch soon from the port of Saint-Nazaire.

However, we must not overlook a direct consequence of a possible relocation: an increase in the price of goods. Consumers may be reluctant to pay more for basic necessities after becoming accustomed to paying less, and may complain about a decline in their purchasing power.

There are no quick fixes, but as with any revolution, there are avenues to be explored. And as the planet's climate suffers an unprecedented crisis, solutions must be sought everywhere. Even if it means dreaming a little . . .

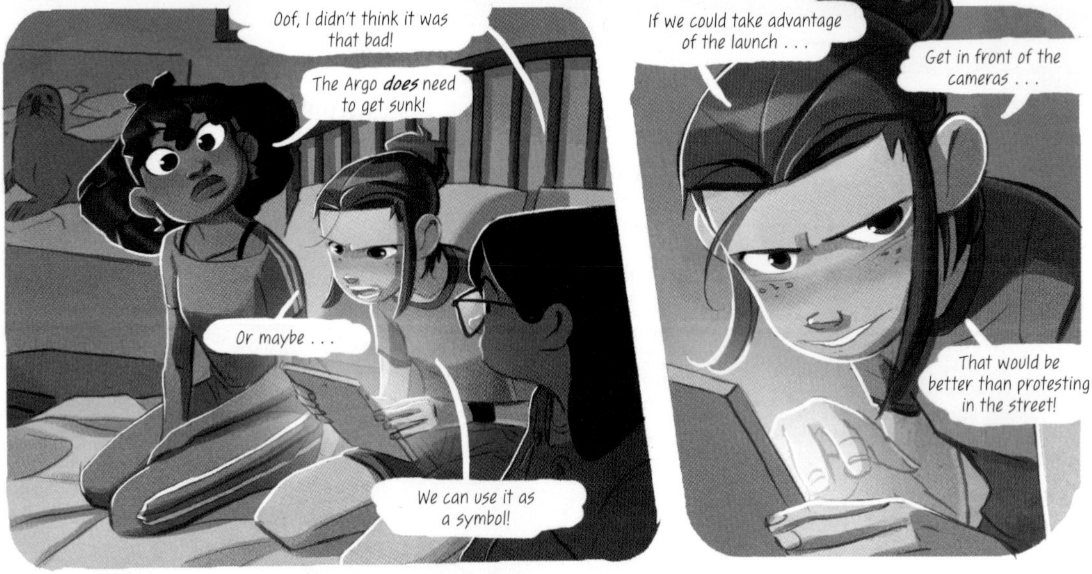
Oof, I didn't think it was that bad!
The Argo **does** need to get sunk!
Or maybe . . .
We can use it as a symbol!
If we could take advantage of the launch . . .
Get in front of the cameras . . .
That would be better than protesting in the street!

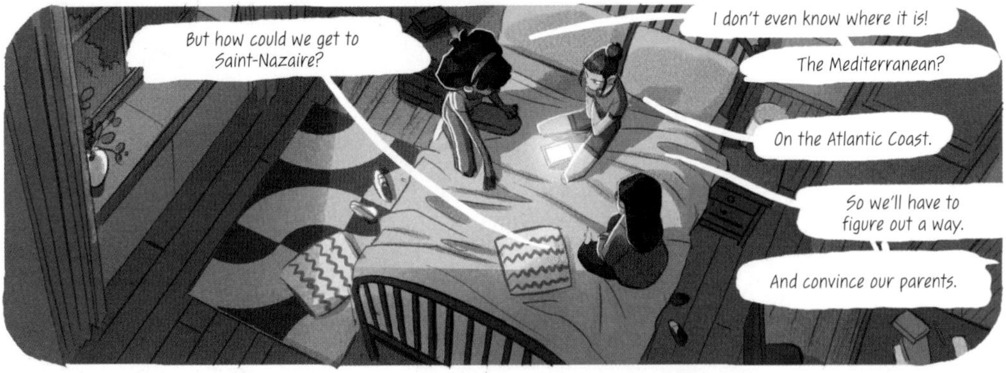
But how could we get to Saint-Nazaire?
I don't even know where it is!
The Mediterranean?
On the Atlantic Coast.
So we'll have to figure out a way.
And convince our parents.

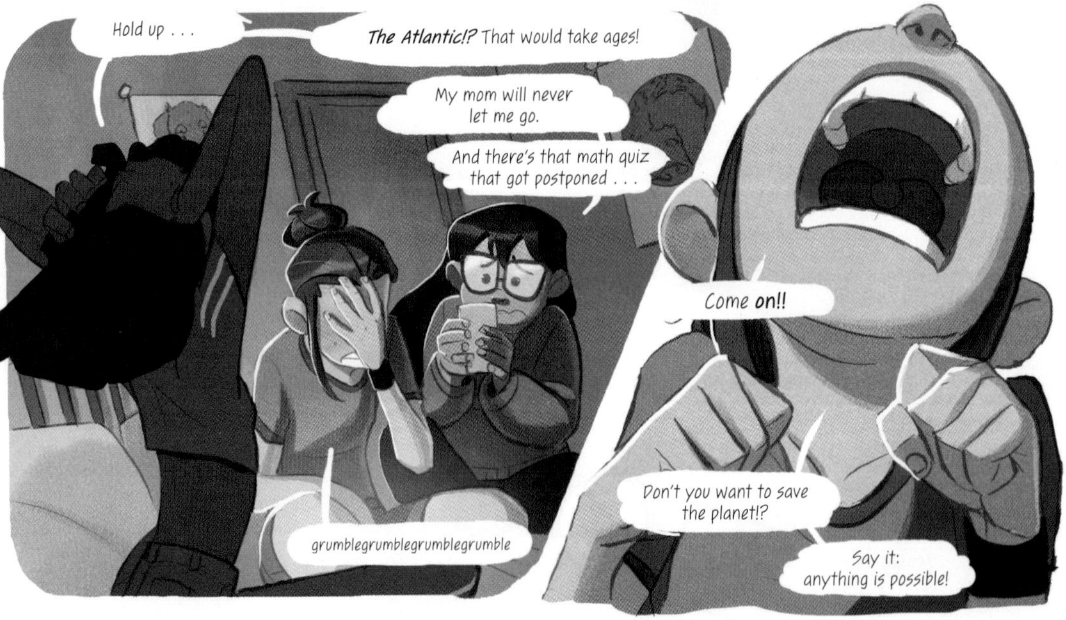
Hold up . . .
The Atlantic!? That would take ages!
My mom will never let me go.
And there's that math quiz that got postponed . . .
grumblegrumblegrumblegrumble
Come **on**!!
Don't you want to save the planet!?
Say it: anything is possible!

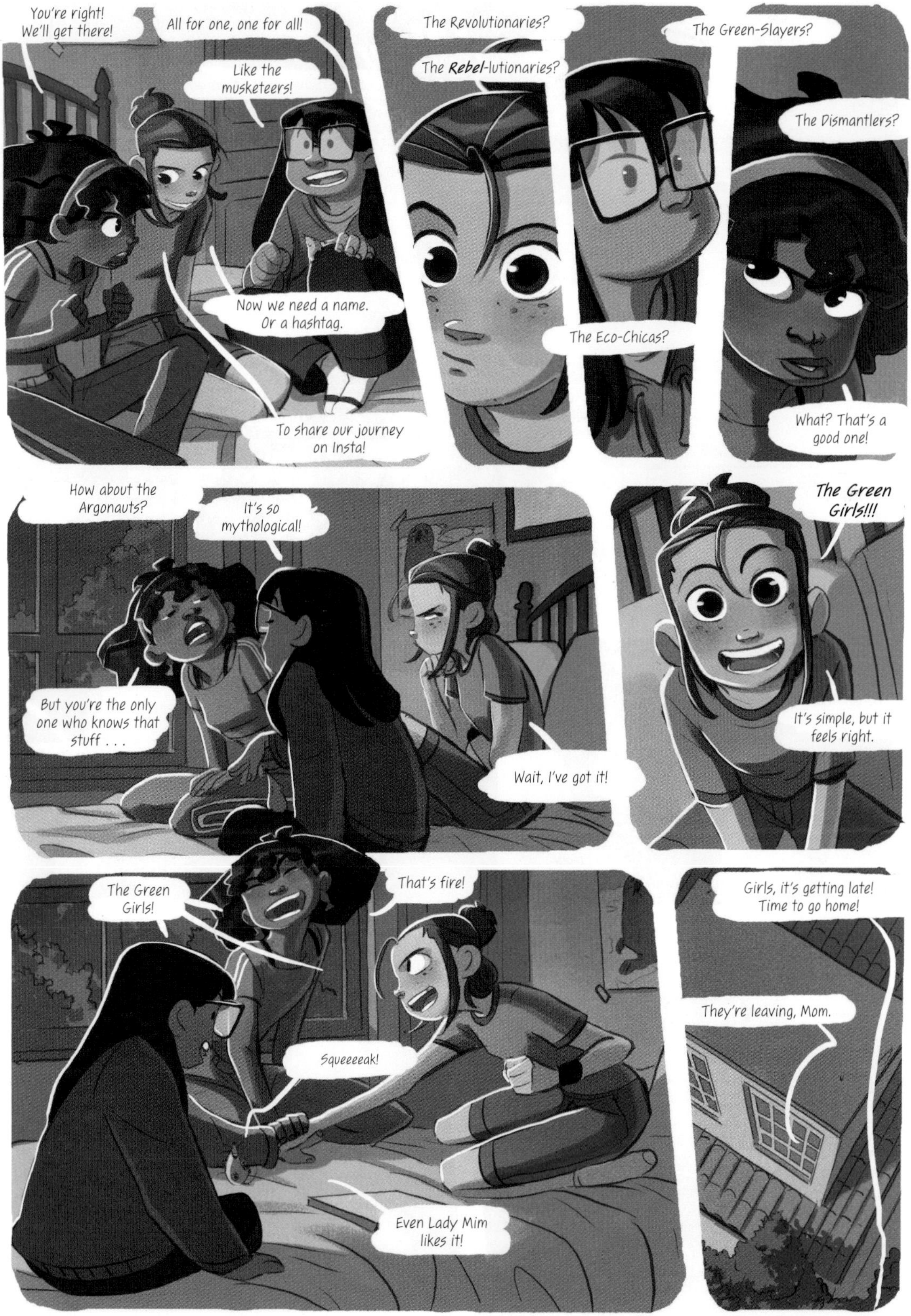
You're right! We'll get there!
All for one, one for all!
Like the musketeers!
Now we need a name. Or a hashtag.
To share our journey on Insta!
The Revolutionaries?
The *Rebel*-lutionaries?
The Eco-Chicas?
The Green-Slayers?
The Dismantlers?
What? That's a good one!
How about the Argonauts?
It's so mythological!
But you're the only one who knows that stuff . . .
Wait, I've got it!
The Green Girls!!!
It's simple, but it feels right.
The Green Girls!
That's fire!
Squeeeeak!
Even Lady Mim likes it!
Girls, it's getting late! Time to go home!
They're leaving, Mom.

Hey girls!

I didn't sleep a wink last night.

I kept thinking about our project.

You're not the only one!

I've outdone myself.

Me too.

I saw that to get access to the boat launch, we'd have to pass ourselves off as superfans.

So I made a blog.

I spent the night writing posts about all kind of boats.

We Stan Ships!
The blog for fans of whatever's on the water!

Can you imagine? Actually, I get really seasick.

Now I just want one thing: some sleep!

So legit, Lily!

And I've planned our entire journey.

Whoa!

It was like everything clicked into place.

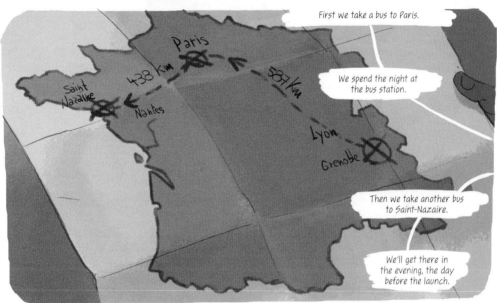

First we take a bus to Paris.

We spend the night at the bus station.

Then we take another bus to Saint-Nazaire.

We'll get there in the evening, the day before the launch.

Paris

438 Km

587 Km

Saint Nazaire

Nantes

Lyon

Grenoble

Fadila, girl, you rock!

Thank you! And it will cost next to nothing.

But it will take **forever**.

Why don't we take a plane?

Seriously? We're fighting ocean pollution and you want to pollute the air?

Where's that piece on planes . . . ?

WHY PUT A CEILING ON FLYING?

For years, environmental groups have opposed the openings of new airports and asked for increases in the taxation of fuel oil, pointing to air pollution. But do we really have to cut down on flying?

The aviation revolution

Between the start of the 20th century and the 21st century, the face of the planet radically changed. The other side of the world, which was many days away by boat, became only a few hours away by plane. Economic and cultural exchanges have been simplified and amplified, and tourism has been a real revolution for many countries. Air traffic has exploded more than any other form of transportation, with international passenger numbers doubling every ten years.

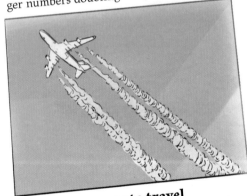

A troubling way to travel

Two main criticisms are leveled at aviation. The first is pollution of the sky. The consumption of heavy fuel oil releases enormous quantities of oxide and ozone in the air, and trails left in the wake of planes spoil pristine skies.

The second is noise pollution, which can disrupt the lives of people who live near airports. Even if pilots reduce engine power during planes' landings, many residents consider this sound unbearable. Finally, even if flying is the safest mode of travel, each accident that happens is catastrophic.

Individual responsibility

The problem is not with aviation itself but with its excessive use. For work or vacations, why take planes for short domestic trips if an efficient train is an option? Why pay for postal transport by plane knowing that, by land, the additional delivery time is negligible?

This is where everyone can make a responsible move: take a train when possible and buy postage at a greener rate. You may laugh at the suggestion, but if everyone does it, it can make a big difference.

That said, the airplane is the fastest and safest way to travel around the world, even if the COVID-19 pandemic has changed the way we travel . . . and the price of tickets!

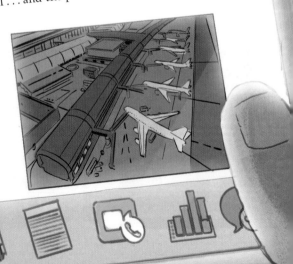

Well . . . it's not *that* bad.

It's not that good either.

We have to be **consistent!**

We can't fight pollution and take planes everywhere!

Ugh. Getting there will be so boring.

Hey, there's one thing we haven't talked about . . .

Our excuse!

It takes two days to get there. So it takes two days to get back.

My parents would never let me be away that long!

Same here.

And how do we swing the nights in Paris and Saint-Nazaire?

I don't sleep under bridges.

And hotels cost a ton.

Wake up! We're not going on vacation . . .

We're going on an *adventure!*

We have to take risks!

So what do we tell our folks?

I have an idea . . .

But I need your help.

A climate protest in Paris?

On Thursday?

Youth for Climate, Uncle Dominic!

There will be young people from all over France!

The heads of the European Union are passing through.

To tell boomers to stop destroying the planet.

Boomers?

Yeah, the old—

Ulp!

People your age.

Come on, Uncle Dom, you know how my mom is.

I don't want her to freak out about us going.

We'll stick together the whole time.

So there's no risk.

If it's in Paris, why don't you stay at my brother's?

At your *dad's* house?

Do you know how long it's been since I've seen him?

Come on, Dom, *pleeease?*

Fiiine.

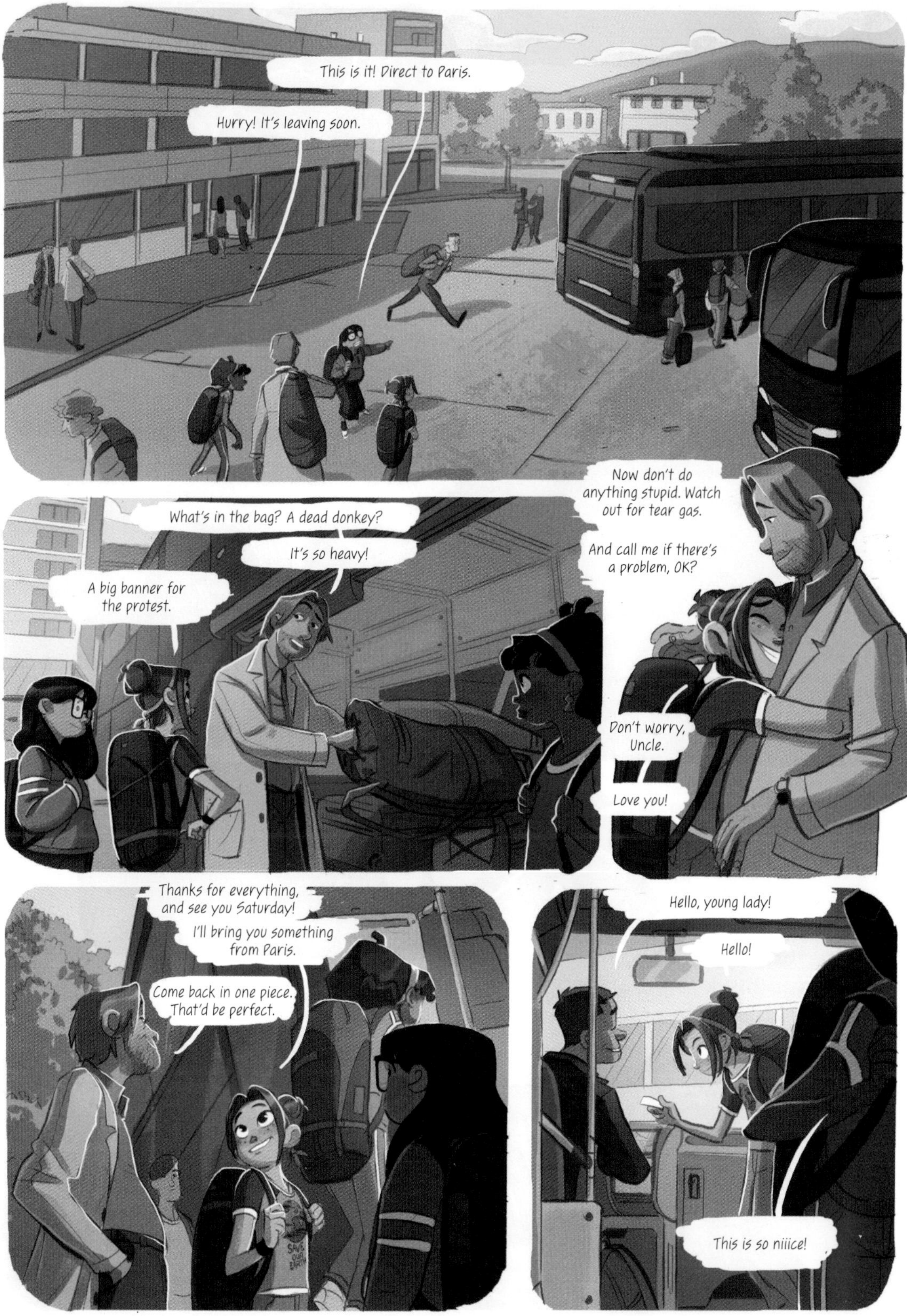
This is it! Direct to Paris.
Hurry! It's leaving soon.
What's in the bag? A dead donkey?
It's so heavy!
A big banner for the protest.
Now don't do anything stupid. Watch out for tear gas.
And call me if there's a problem, OK?
Don't worry, Uncle.
Love you!
Thanks for everything, and see you Saturday!
I'll bring you something from Paris.
Come back in one piece. That'd be perfect.
Hello, young lady!
Hello!
This is so niiice!

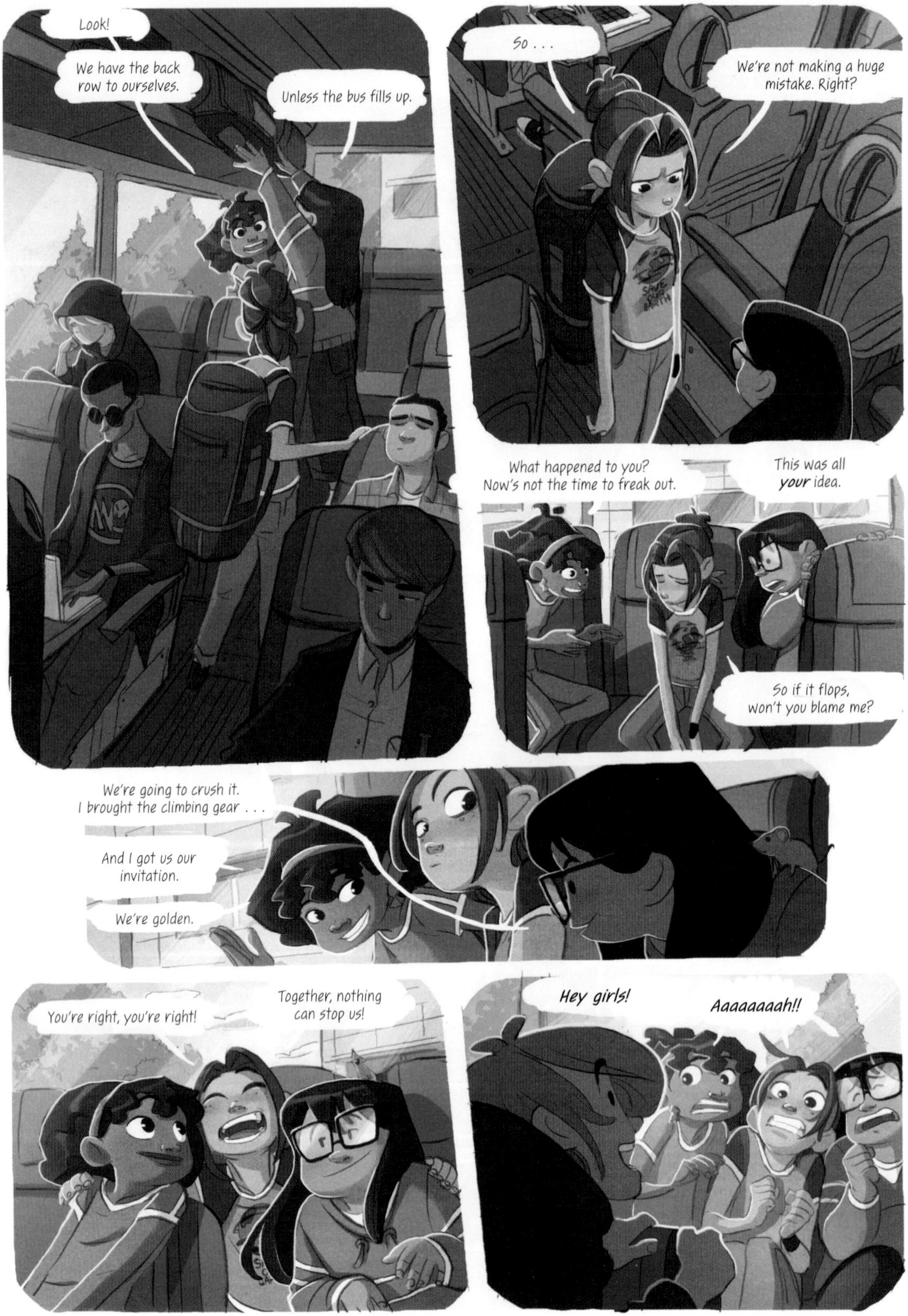
Look!
We have the back row to ourselves.
Unless the bus fills up.
So . . .
We're not making a huge mistake. Right?
What happened to you? Now's not the time to freak out.
This was all **your** idea.
So if it flops, won't you blame me?
We're going to crush it. I brought the climbing gear . . .
And I got us our invitation.
We're golden.
You're right, you're right!
Together, nothing can stop us!
Hey girls!
Aaaaaaaah!!

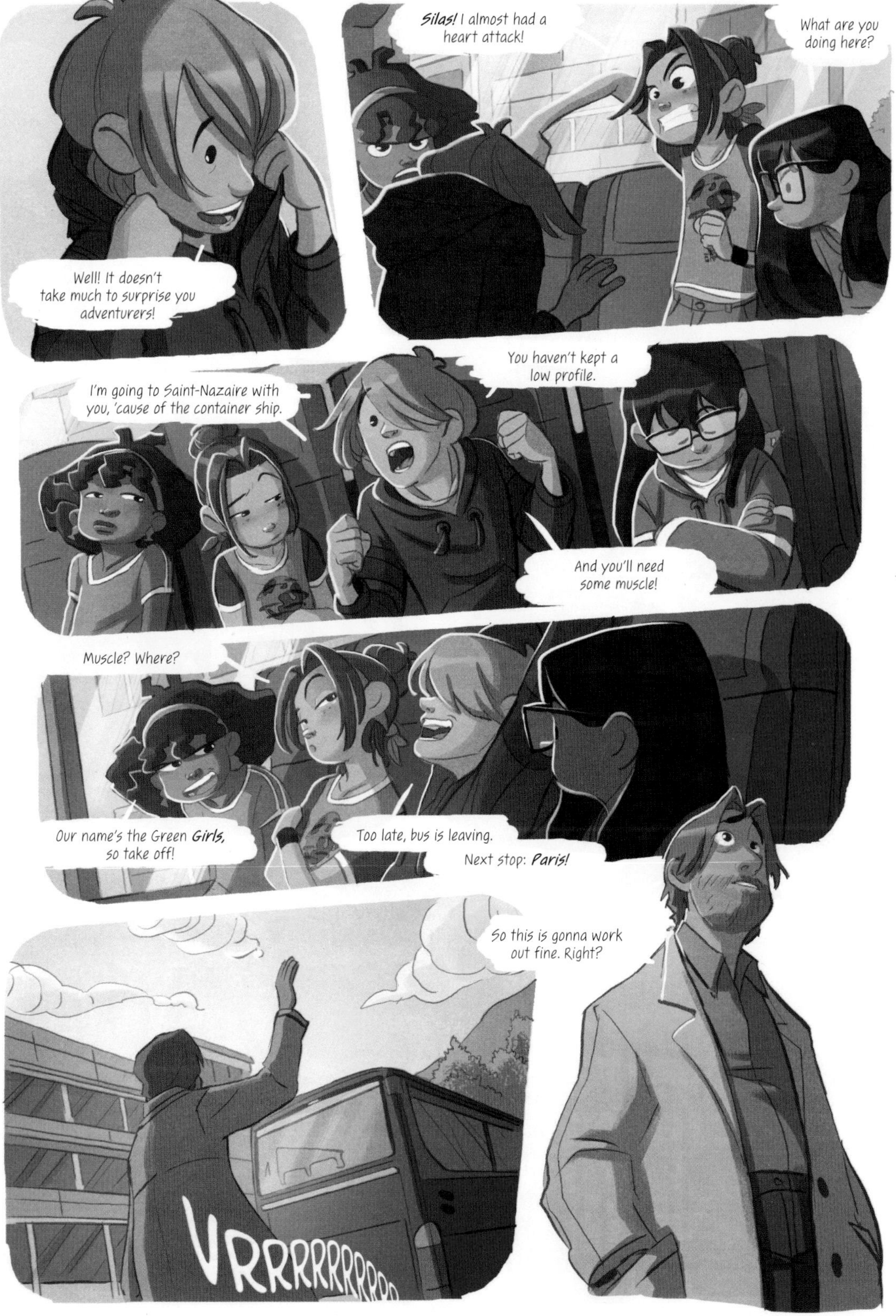
Well! It doesn't take much to surprise you adventurers!
Silas! I almost had a heart attack!
What are you doing here?
I'm going to Saint-Nazaire with you, 'cause of the container ship.
You haven't kept a low profile.
And you'll need some muscle!
Muscle? Where?
Our name's the Green Girls, so take off!
Too late, bus is leaving.
Next stop: Paris!
So this is gonna work out fine. Right?
VRRRRRRRRRO

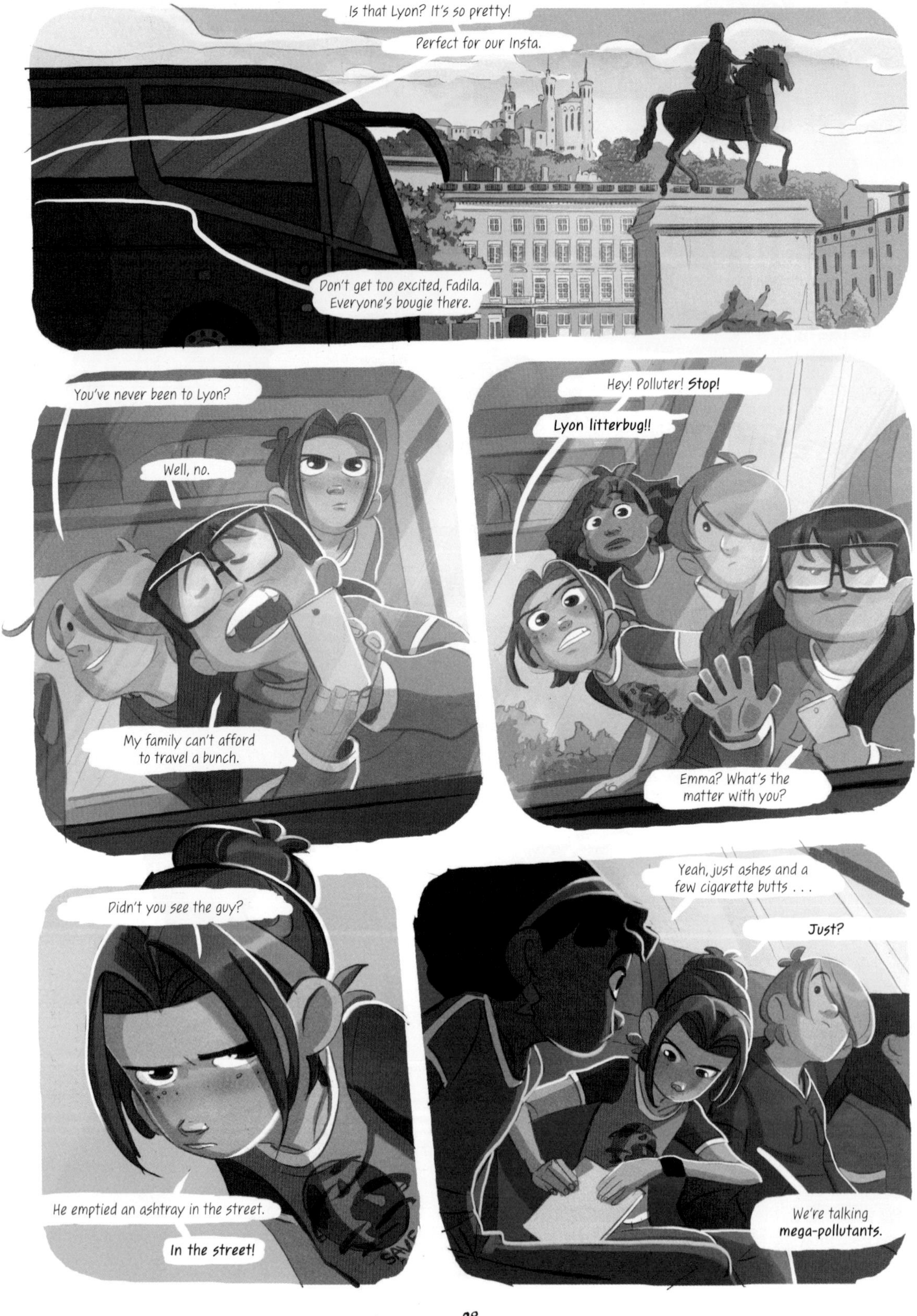
Is that Lyon? It's so pretty!
Perfect for our Insta.
Don't get too excited, Fadila. Everyone's bougie there.
You've never been to Lyon?
Well, no.
My family can't afford to travel a bunch.
Hey! Polluter! **Stop!**
Lyon litterbug!!
Emma? What's the matter with you?
Didn't you see the guy?
He emptied an ashtray in the street.
In the street!
Yeah, just ashes and a few cigarette butts . . .
Just?
We're talking **mega-pollutants.**

CIGARETTE BUTTS: AN UNDERESTIMATED POLLUTANT

Tossing a butt on the street: a small act, and a habit (within a habit) that smokers find hard to break. But if they knew the consequences, maybe they would think twice.

An ecological disaster

On every cigarette produced in the world, there is a filter made of plastics and about fifty toxic components. It will completely break down in between two and 10 years. In France alone, the number of cigarette butts thrown in the street is estimated at 40 billion per year, or nearly 25 tons.

Here's what you might not expect: cigarette butts thrown on the ground in cities or in nature mostly end up in rivers and seas. They have incredible polluting power: a single cigarette can contaminate 500 liters of water. Researchers have even demonstrated that fish die in water polluted by only two butts per liter of water.

A challenge for smokers

There are already many initiatives (dedicated bins; no-smoking parks, beaches, and streets) and fines, but individual smokers must be vigilant too. Throw butts in the trash or in portable ashtrays. It's not rocket science. A little effort and a new habit would make a big difference for the planet!

A dangerous action

Throwing your butt in the street or abandoning it on a beach is a sign of disregard for your fellow citizens. And what about the drivers who throw their butts out the window into nature? Every year, dozens of fires start this way: with reckless citizens who do not reflect on their actions. Not to mention that, to continue the global consumption of cigarettes, people cut down almost 495,000 acres of forest per year for the cultivation of tobacco.

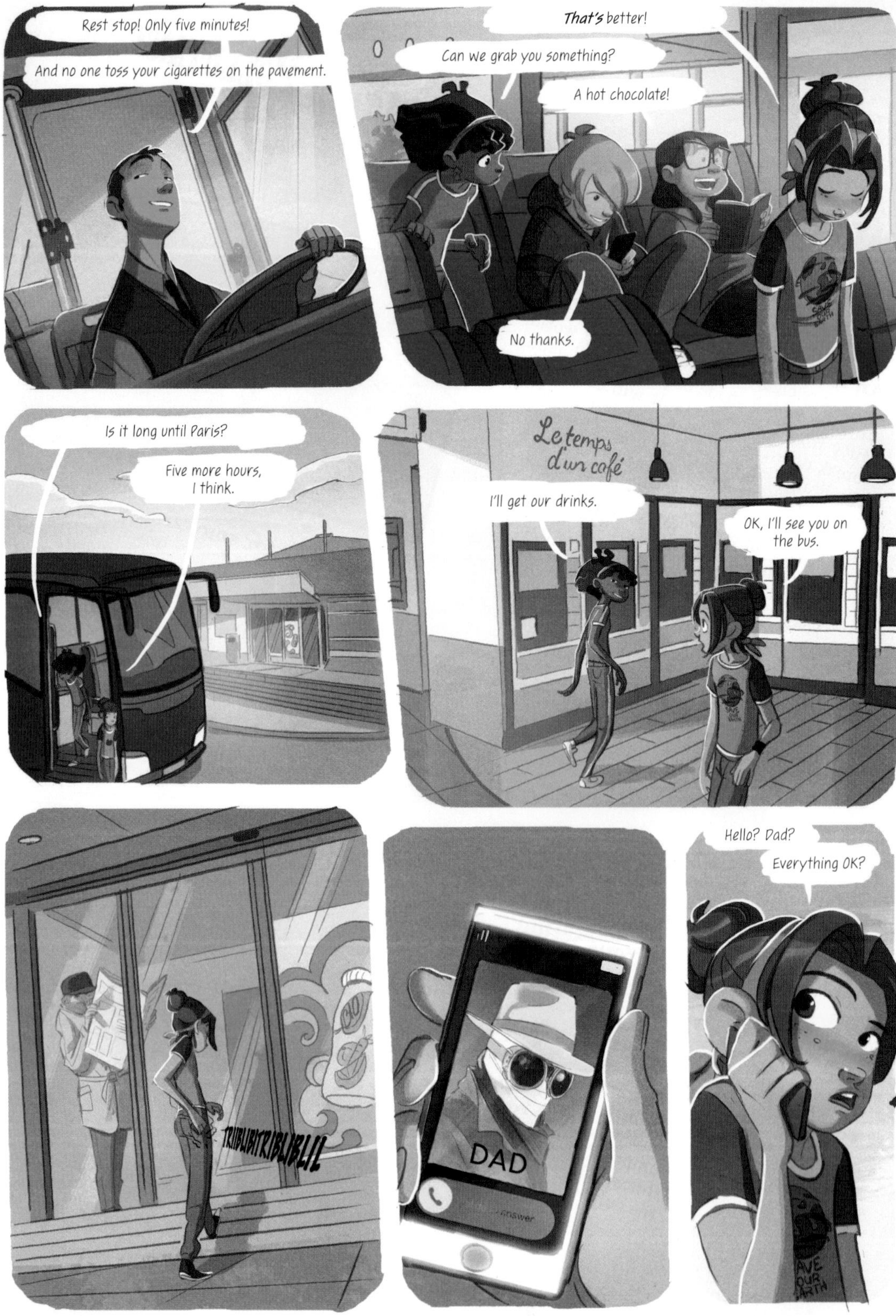

Rest stop! Only five minutes!
And no one toss your cigarettes on the pavement.
That's better!
Can we grab you something?
A hot chocolate!
No thanks.
Is it long until Paris?
Five more hours, I think.
Le temps d'un café
I'll get our drinks.
OK, I'll see you on the bus.
TRIIBLIBITRIBLIBLIL
DAD
answer
Hello? Dad?
Everything OK?
SAVE OUR EARTH

Sorry, this is his assistant.

He has an opening in ten days. Will you be free?

I think so.

For the weekend?

So sorry. His schedule is quite busy.

He can see you at Grenoble station for half an hour.

Would that work?

Oh. Sure.

Perfect. I'll add it to his calendar.

Thank you, and have a nice day.

You too.

Emma!

What are you doing!?

The bus!!

Heyyyyyyy!!

Back here!

See? I told you they were coming!

OK, OK, I'm stopping!

KKKKRRRRRIIIIIII

Sorry! Didn't see time rushing by.

Next time, I'm not stopping!

I have schedules to keep!

You scared the heck out of us! We couldn't find you!

Everything OK, Emma?

I'm good.

Can't wait till we get to Paris.

What's the plan?

Can we find a place to sleep in the station?

I told you I planned out everything.

We put the big bag in the locker.

Next, we take the Metro.

This one's self-driving!

I'm hallucinating. A driverless train!

Hope the computer at the controls doesn't short-circuit!

We went all the way across Paris, huh?

METROPOLITAIN

Almost. *This* is our real introduction to . . .

The finest sight in town!

!!!

33

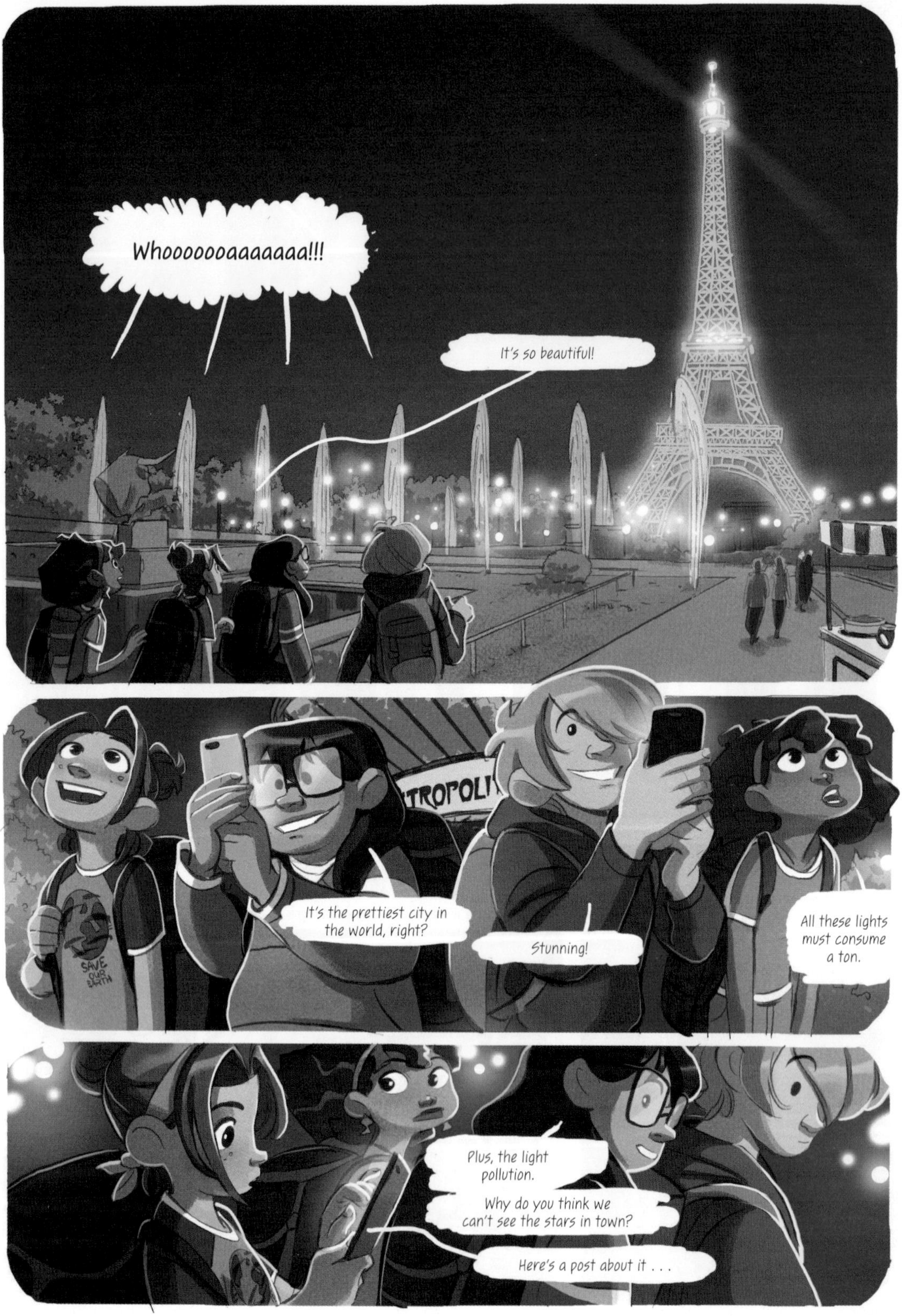

Whoooooaaaaaaa!!!
It's so beautiful!
TROPOLI
It's the prettiest city in the world, right?
Stunning!
All these lights must consume a ton.
SAVE OUR EARTH
Plus, the light pollution.
Why do you think we can't see the stars in town?
Here's a post about it . . .

AS BRIGHT AS DAYLIGHT—AT NIGHT!

For years, environmental groups have complained about a growing phenomenon in metropolitan areas: light pollution.

Defining light pollution

From streetlights to billboards to commercial signs, any light source can prevent you from having a real dark night.

In recent years, some laws have started to recognize the nuisance of artificial lighting, which affects fauna, flora, and people in its disruption of ecosystems. It can impact large areas—and many millions of people who can no longer observe the Milky Way with the naked eye.

These nuisances can disturb human biorhythms due to the absence of a natural shift between day and night. They also generate significant energy costs without being essential. (Note that LED bulbs consume much less and make smaller impacts on national energy consumption.)

Ways to fight the problem

What complicates the situation is that nighttime lighting in residential areas gives many people a feeling of security, even if statistics on crime in many areas suggest that the current amount is unnecessary. People also often appreciate nighttime lighting for aesthetic reasons, particularly when it shines on landmarks or monuments in cities.

The main goal of the fight against light pollution is to assess communities' levels of needs for nighttime lighting and to station lights differently, reducing the negative impacts on our lives.

Advocates for change recommend that some areas turn off their lights at night (from midnight to six in the morning) or alternate the lighting of different areas, and that stores and shopping centers turn off their signs outside of business hours. They also recommend that safety considerations determine the lighting of dangerous roads and alleys.

However, even if many discussions are underway, people are unlikely to see the stars above them in typical city centers.

OK, I get it . . .

But the city's still pretty at night!

One sec, it's my mom.

TRIBLIBIBLIBIBLI

Mom! How nice to hear from you!

Things are going good! Just having a . . . milkshake with the girls!

Oh, and Uncle Dominic, of course!

Big kisses, Mom! Bye!

It's *my* mom!

TRIBLTRIBLTRIBLTRIBL

TRIBLTRIBLTRIBLTRIBL

Mine too! Did they compare notes?

What did you tell *your* parents?

Oh, my dad's not around that much . . .

I don't think he cares what I do!

That's rough.

But I think I have a solution!

A chocolate crepe!

The ultimate pick-me-up.

Hah, sure, Emma.

METROP

Thanks, and if *you* ever want to talk . . .

I'm here to listen.

Aw, you're sweet, Silas.

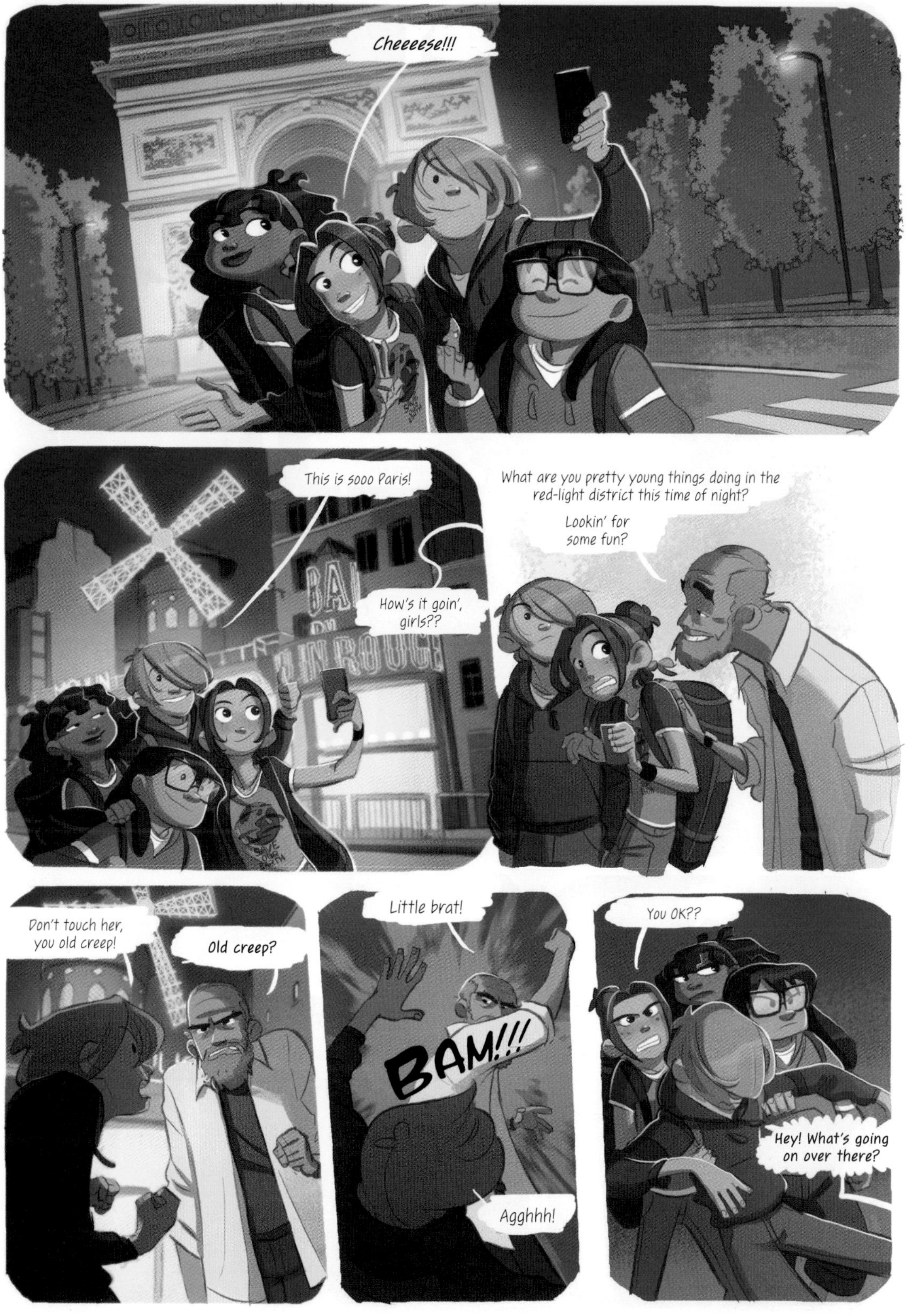
Cheeeese!!!
This is sooo Paris!
How's it goin', girls??
What are you pretty young things doing in the red-light district this time of night?
Lookin' for some fun?
Don't touch her, you old creep!
Old creep?
Little brat!
BAM!!!
Agghhh!
You OK??
Hey! What's going on over there?

What's going on here, sir?

Nothing! Nothing at all!

I was just chatting with these young people . . .

That's not true! He started bothering us . . .

He even hit Silas!

OK, let's see some identification.

Ma'am, c'mon!

You really believe these kids?

And you kids— what are you doing around here at this hour?

???

Wait, where did they go?

Yeah, probably best not to stick around!

Back to the station, quick!

How do you get into *so much* trouble?

It's my rotten karma!

38

ZZZZZZZZZ ZZZZZZZ

TRIBLIILIIBLIDIBLIII

Hey! Wake up! It's here!

And the bus won't wait for us!

You know what's cool about buses?

You can sleep in them . . .

SAINT-NAZAIRE

Does your cheek hurt? It's all swollen.

I'm OK! I felt a lot worse when I broke my leg skiing.

Thank you for helping us.

I wasn't trying to be tough . . . but I had to do something.

Next stop . . . *Saint-Nazaire!*

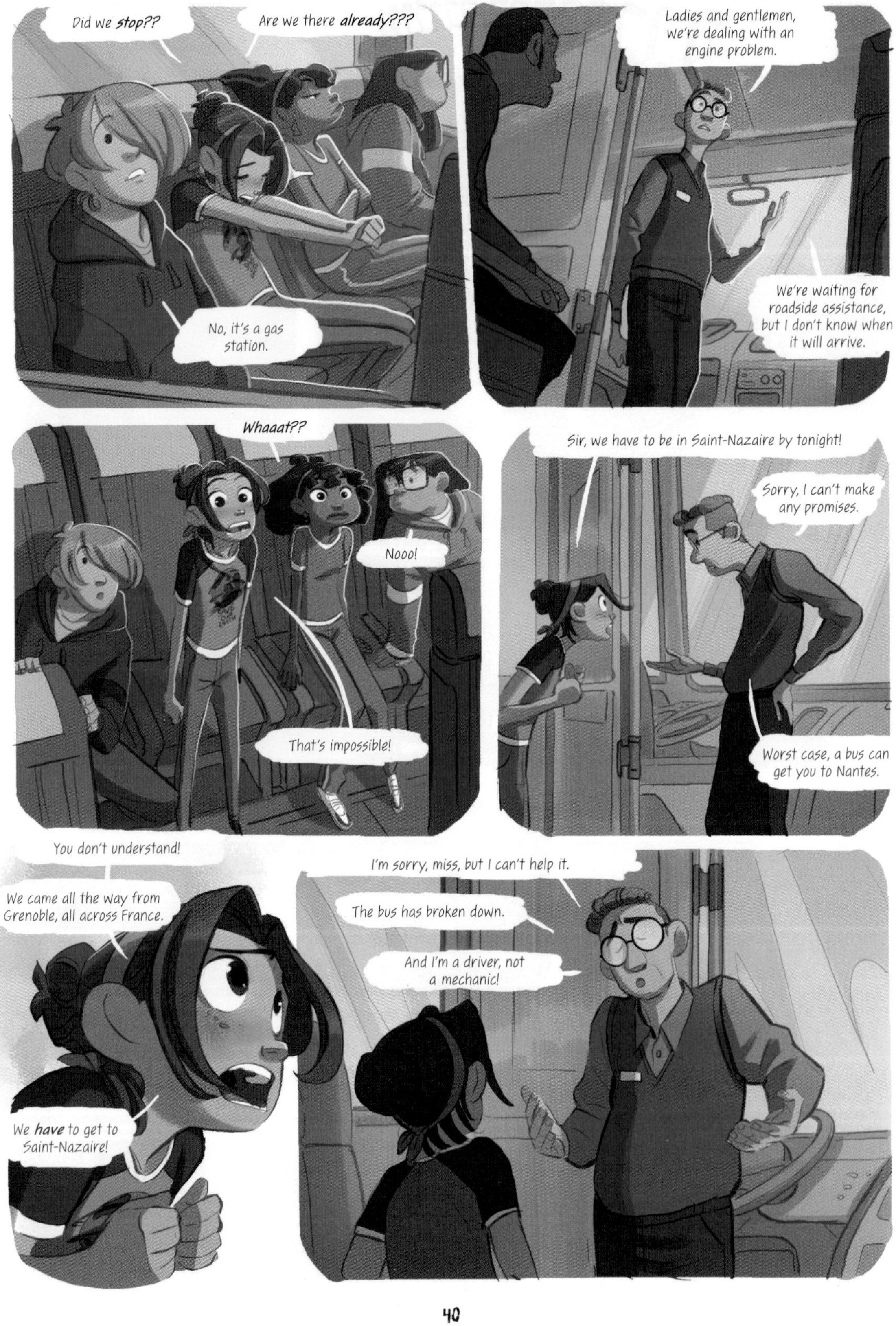
Did we *stop??*
Are we there ***already???***
No, it's a gas station.
Ladies and gentlemen, we're dealing with an engine problem.
We're waiting for roadside assistance, but I don't know when it will arrive.
Whaaat??
Nooo!
That's impossible!
Sir, we have to be in Saint-Nazaire by tonight!
Sorry, I can't make any promises.
Worst case, a bus can get you to Nantes.
You don't understand!
We came all the way from Grenoble, all across France.
We ***have*** to get to Saint-Nazaire!
I'm sorry, miss, but I can't help it.
The bus has broken down.
And I'm a driver, not a mechanic!

What do we do?

We have to find a car to take us!

Let's split up and ask around.

We can't exactly push the bus.

Are you going to Saint-Nazaire?

Nope, Bécherel, in Brittany. Sorry.

Sorry, I only have two free seats.

No no no! I don't want any kids causing me any trouble!

Sure, hon, I'm going to Saint-Nazaire.

I have four seats too.

You're *the best*, ma'am. I'll just . . .

Oh my God!
What is that little horror!?

I hate rats!!!

But she's a shrew!

And really sweet.

Well this plan's dead in the water.

Dead, dead, dead.

We asked everybody . . .

So what do we do now?

I didn't cross the country for nothing!

We should never have followed your dumb plan.

???

It was just a little bad luck . . .

Dumb plan? Hey, listen . . .

I didn't *force* you to come.

You said you'd planned for everything!

Now we're stuck at a gas station!

It's easy to criticize me when you don't *do anything!*

You just moan all the time!

At least *I* have a dad who loves me!

I don't have to do stupid stuff to make him notice me!

Everybody chill for a sec, OK??

This isn't the time for arguing . . .

Oh, forget it!

I'll get to Saint-Nazaire *alone!*

I don't need dead weight on my back.

You were a little harsh there.

You have to be firm sometimes.

Wait, who's Emma's dad?

All I need is a lift.

Then I'll show 'em . . .

Hey, kid!

What's a pretty girl like you doing out here?

Ugh, not another creep!

Back off, or I'll . . .

Creep? Me?

I thought you'd be happy for the help!

Dominic!?

I think I'm freaking out.

Yeah, I can tell.

What are you doing here?

Just playing my role as chaperone.

I followed you from Grenoble!

You lost me at the Metro station in Paris . . .

So I hung by the station lockers.

You're the best uncle in the world!

Mostly I don't want to get yelled at by your mom.

But you're all right too.

Now let's find your friends!

You all need to explain what you're trying to do in Saint-Nazaire.

Surpriiise!!!

Dominic? What's he doing here?

We'll explain in the car.

He's our ride to Saint-Nazaire.

Emma, I'm kicking myself for what I said.

I'm the dummy!

You know, it really hurt.

But we Green Girls forgive each other!

Yeah? Cool!

Well said!

We are *the Green Girls!*

And we're stronger together!

That's sweet and all, but we should go.

Let's move, girls . . .

And, uh, Silas.

There you have it! The Saint-Nazaire Bridge.

Impressive, huh?

Whoo! So pretty.

It'll blow up on Insta.

Fadila, what's the matter? Are you crying?

It's my first time seeing the ocean!

It's beautiful.

And there's the mouth of the Loire!

We'll get an even better look at the ocean tomorrow.

So this is for what, a presentation?

That's why you're going to a ship launch?

Yes, for Mrs. Berenger's class.

Our presentation's called . . .

Uh, the title is . . .

???

What's she talking about?

She had to tell her uncle a tiny lie . . .

"Modern Monsters that Float on the Water"!

Yep! Right. That's it.

Huh, interesting.

You'll have to record the presentation—I want to see it!

Now, anybody hungry?

How about ice cream at the harbor?

Yeah!!

47

Yeah, they're all safe and enjoying themselves!

What?

Mmmmmmmmm!!

I promise, sis!

I'll bring her back in one piece!

Did you tell my mom we're in Saint-Nazaire?

You want her to kill me? No! We're just skiing.

Now I just have to call Fadila's mom.

So how many followers are we up to on Insta?

Apart from our solo accounts . . . none. But just wait!

You should do more videos!

You're right! Get a clip of the biggest scoop of ice cream anyone's ever eaten.

Not too many videos.

You have no idea the carbon footprint those leave.

I think I saved an article on that . . .

The Internet: Game Changer or Polluter?

Since its inception, the internet has revolutionized communication across the planet, with an often-overlooked consequence: the explosion of digital pollution. An alarming finding?

If you click? You pollute.

Checking our social networking apps, sending messages, posting photos and videos, and storing documents online are small things, and we don't always wonder about their energy costs. But in order to function, the servers and cables that make up the internet network consume energy—and through that, they pollute!

For example, sending a simple email of a few kilobytes corresponds to 20 grams of CO_2 released into the atmosphere. And the number of emails exchanged per year is estimated at 250 billion. The math is simple, and the result is colossal!

So imagine the amounts of information circulating on the internet when you take into account the audio or video data from all streaming platforms. The global data traffic in 2019 was estimated at 2 zettabytes (2,000 billion gigabytes) . . . a figure that makes your head spin. In France, the Ecological Transition Agency estimates that 14 percent of the energy produced is consumed by electronic devices.

Data centers: energy pits

At the heart of the controversy are data centers, or hubs: farms of servers with enormous calculation and information-processing power. While operating, they consume a lot of energy, as do the air-conditioning units that must absorb the immense heat these devices give off.

To reduce the energy consumption of these buildings, operators are making efforts to supply the servers with green energy (from nearby wind turbines) and installing green roofs or alternative cooling systems. But that will never be enough if the use of these data centers does not decrease.

A few small, simple gestures

To reduce your carbon footprint, here are some simple tips:

- **Don't charge your phone overnight.** Even after your device finishes charging, the transformer still consumes energy.
- **Unsubscribe from newsletters that you don't read.** Try not to send large attachments to too many people. And delete unnecessary emails from your inbox.
- **On streaming platforms, avoid letting audio and video play continuously.** If possible, disable automatic next play.
- **Decrease the resolution of videos.** There's usually no need to watch a clip in 4K or HD, especially on your phone, where a 360p resolution is more than sufficient.

Seriously??

So we're *also* big polluters?

'Fraid so! It's not just big companies.

Everybody's gotta make some changes.

Yep, there's waste all around.

Hear that, Mim? Let's take it easy with the whipped cream.

You're freaking me out, Fadila. You sound like your mom.

Ha ha ha ha!

OK, your moms are officially reassured.

All that's left to find a small hotel . . .

Ta-daa. I got two rooms, side by side.

One for the girls, one for us guys.

Sleep well and be ready to rise and shine.

Night, girls!

Good night!!

50

So what now? Our plan's ruined.

If he's right next door, he'll hear us come out.

And what if he checks on us?

We have to stay here!

This is no time to flip out.

I've got it covered!

Come on, let's hustle!

The port's not exactly next door.

You even brought wire cutters?

What did I say? I got this!

All these containers . . .

It's like a maze.

There it is, girls!

The Argo!

Whooaaa!!!

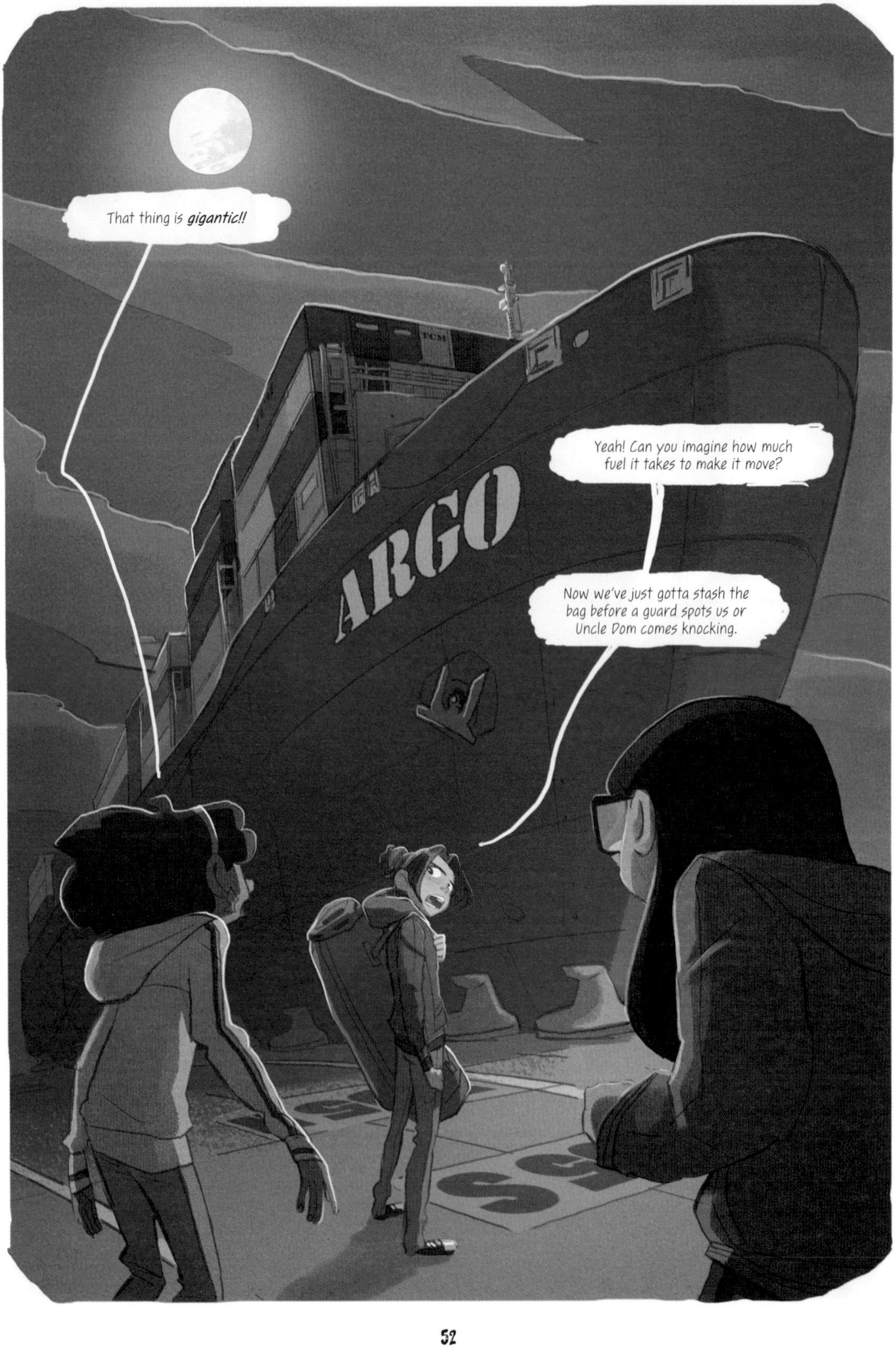
That thing is *gigantic!!*
ARGO
Yeah! Can you imagine how much fuel it takes to make it move?
Now we've just gotta stash the bag before a guard spots us or Uncle Dom comes knocking.

Before I turn in, I'll make sure the girls are OK.

You sure?

They might already be sleeping. They were pretty beat.

207

KNOCK KNOCK KNOCK

Hey girls, it's Dominic!

Everything good?

Dominic's outside your room! I couldn't stop him.

Answer, quick!

Girls? I can't hear you.

Is there a problem?

No no, we're good!

I can't be too loud. Lily and Fadila are already asleep.

Oh, sorry. I'll let you be.

Good night, Uncle!

That's that!

Huh. A walkie-talkie app!

ARGO

But we really shouldn't stick around.

Uhh . . . girls?

You awake?

We're going down to breakfast.

You coming?

Yeah, yeah, for sure . . .

But . . . what time is it?

It's 9:00 a.m.??

Noooo!!

Guys! It's nine o'clock!

We're seriously late!!

Hmm . . . nine o'clock . . .

Nine o'clock!!!

Well, well, they're finally awake!

Sorry, Dom . . .

Getting up was hard!

Since I didn't see you down there . . .

I grabbed you stuff from the breakfast buffet.

Oh, you're a sweetheart, Silas!

There you have it! We're here.

I'll park and join you.

OK, Dom, see you soon.

All right, we're almost at the finish line! Everyone have an ID card?

Lily, what should we say?

Don't worry, I've got it.

Hello, sir. We're here for the launch.

We're from the blog *We Stan Ships*.

Yes, you're on the list. Three passes.

Oh, but our photographer's here too!

Is there any way to also get him in?

Contact the press secretary.

Does . . . this mean I'm going home?

Get out your camera and don't worry.

Lily can reel in anyone . . .

Oh, how wonderful!

I'm so happy you've come!

It's so rare to find young people interested in our ships.

Thank you so much, but I forgot to mention . . .

With Silas here, there are four of us. He's the best photographer in our middle school!

Ah. That might be complicated . . .

But we'll make it work!

On the condition you post a very "lit" piece about the launch.

Here are your press passes. Don't lose them.

Cool.

Stylish!

Hey, what about Dominic?

Well, Silas was already tricky . . .

Sorry, Uncle Dom.

We couldn't get you a pass.

Don't worry, no big deal.

I've got a good view of the boat from here!

I can't believe it! We're in!

Go ahead, I'll wait by the car.

See you soon!

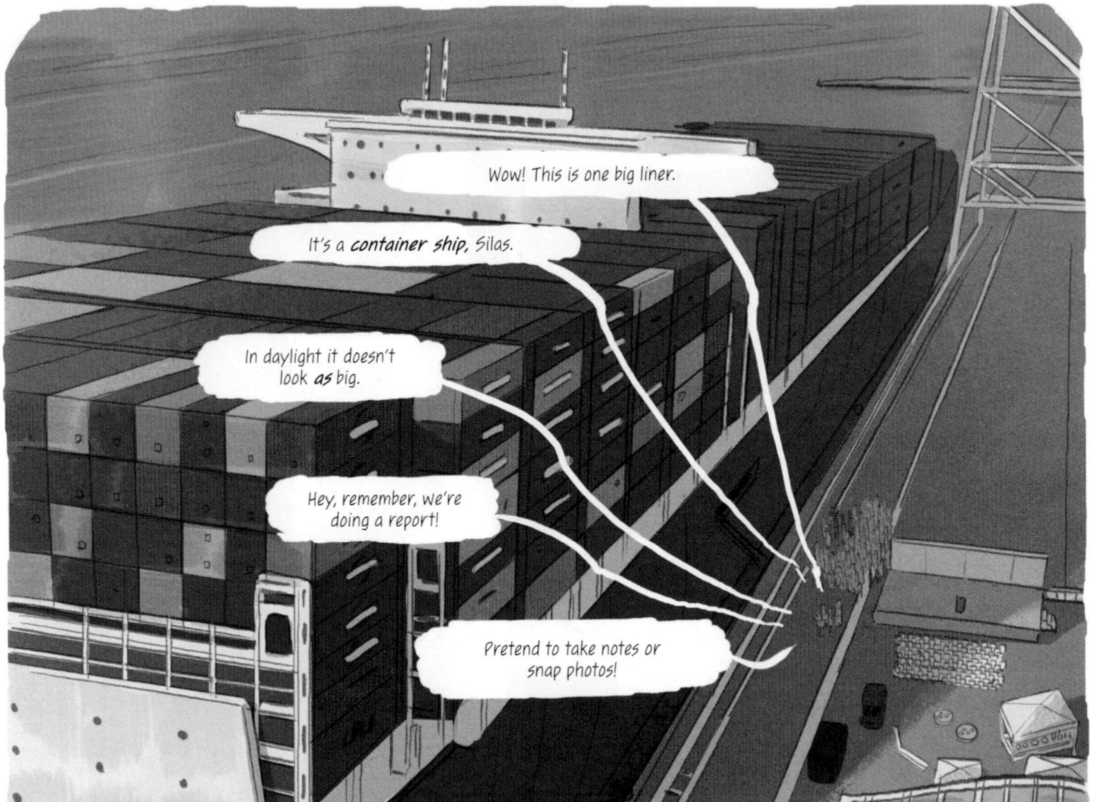
Wow! This is one big liner.
It's a **container ship,** Silas.
In daylight it doesn't look *as* big.
Hey, remember, we're doing a report!
Pretend to take notes or snap photos!

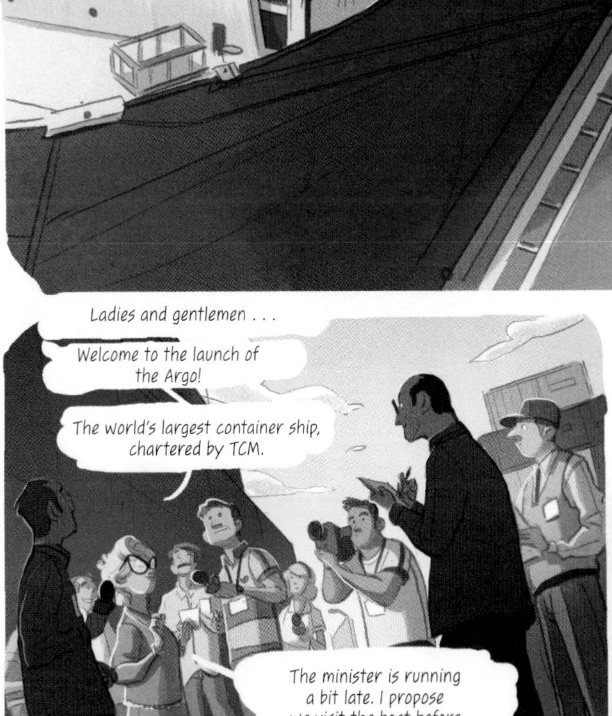
Ladies and gentlemen . . .
Welcome to the launch of the Argo!
The world's largest container ship, chartered by TCM.
The minister is running a bit late. I propose we visit the boat before his speech.

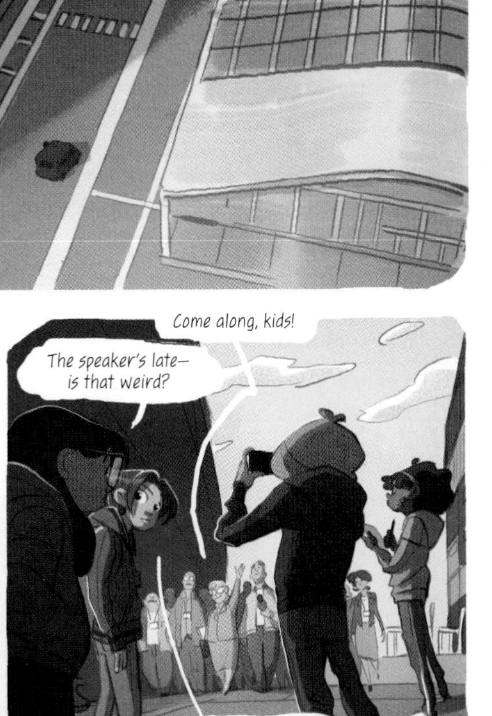
Come along, kids!
The speaker's late—is that weird?
If he comes at all, that's a first.

Watch your step! The stairs are a little slippery.

Please nobody break a leg after traveling across the whole country.

So what *is* your plan?

We split from the tour at the turn of a hallway.

We hid the bag with the banner and the leaflets just under the platform!

Follow me closely. We could lose each other fast in such a big ship.

Now we'll head to the pilot station. The view is breathtaking!

Ready . . .

Go!!!

This way . . .

Does everyone know what they're doing?

As soon as we get there, we put up the banner . . .

And take out the leaflets!

You *sure* this is the way?

Obviously! What do you take me for?

The engine room! Pretty impressive.

But I don't recognize the way.

Emma, are we already lost?

It's OK! It's just a little maze-like.

All these machines—it's wild.

If we could put all this know-how toward saving the planet . . .

Let's go back up and take a right . . .

Now, I think the bridge is just below.

Stop! We *know* you're lost.

And like that, we're—

???

What are you doing here?

This is a restricted area!

Where's your authorization?

Quick, girls, turn around!

Stop!

You won't get far!

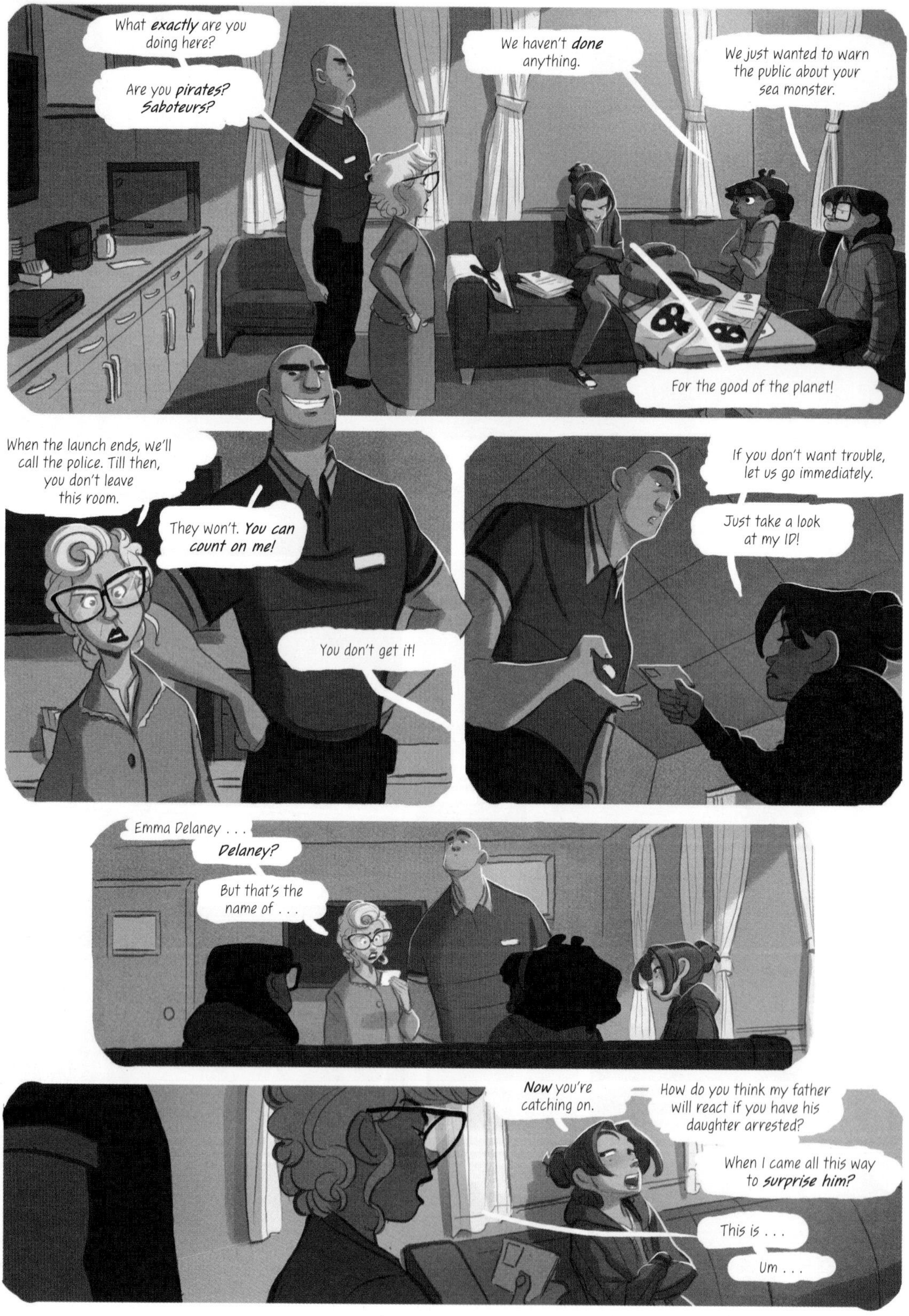
What **exactly** are you doing here?
Are you **pirates? Saboteurs?**
We haven't **done** anything.
We just wanted to warn the public about your sea monster.
For the good of the planet!
When the launch ends, we'll call the police. Till then, you don't leave this room.
They won't. **You can count on me!**
You don't get it!
If you don't want trouble, let us go immediately.
Just take a look at my ID!
Emma Delaney . . .
Delaney?
But that's the name of . . .
Now you're catching on.
How do you think my father will react if you have his daughter arrested?
When I came all this way to **surprise him?**
This is . . .
Um . . .

What a mix-up!

Please don't tell your father . . . ?

We'll have to see . . .

Run! Now! I'll hold them!

I got the banner ready!

That's our muscle!

Come on! You two can smooch later!

Arghh! You won't hold us for long!!

The minister will arrive any minute! I have to welcome him!!

Huh?

Sorry, sir! We're just a little late.

Am I dreaming . . .

. . . or is that *my brother?*

So we're basically right next door.

You sure?

Lily, you tie the cords.

Fadila, you grab the leaflets.

I'll strap myself in!

OK!!!

Thank you for coming, Minister.

I had to be here!

It's a big day for France.

Proof of our industrial muscle.

There we go!

Just gotta squeeze . . .

Stop!!

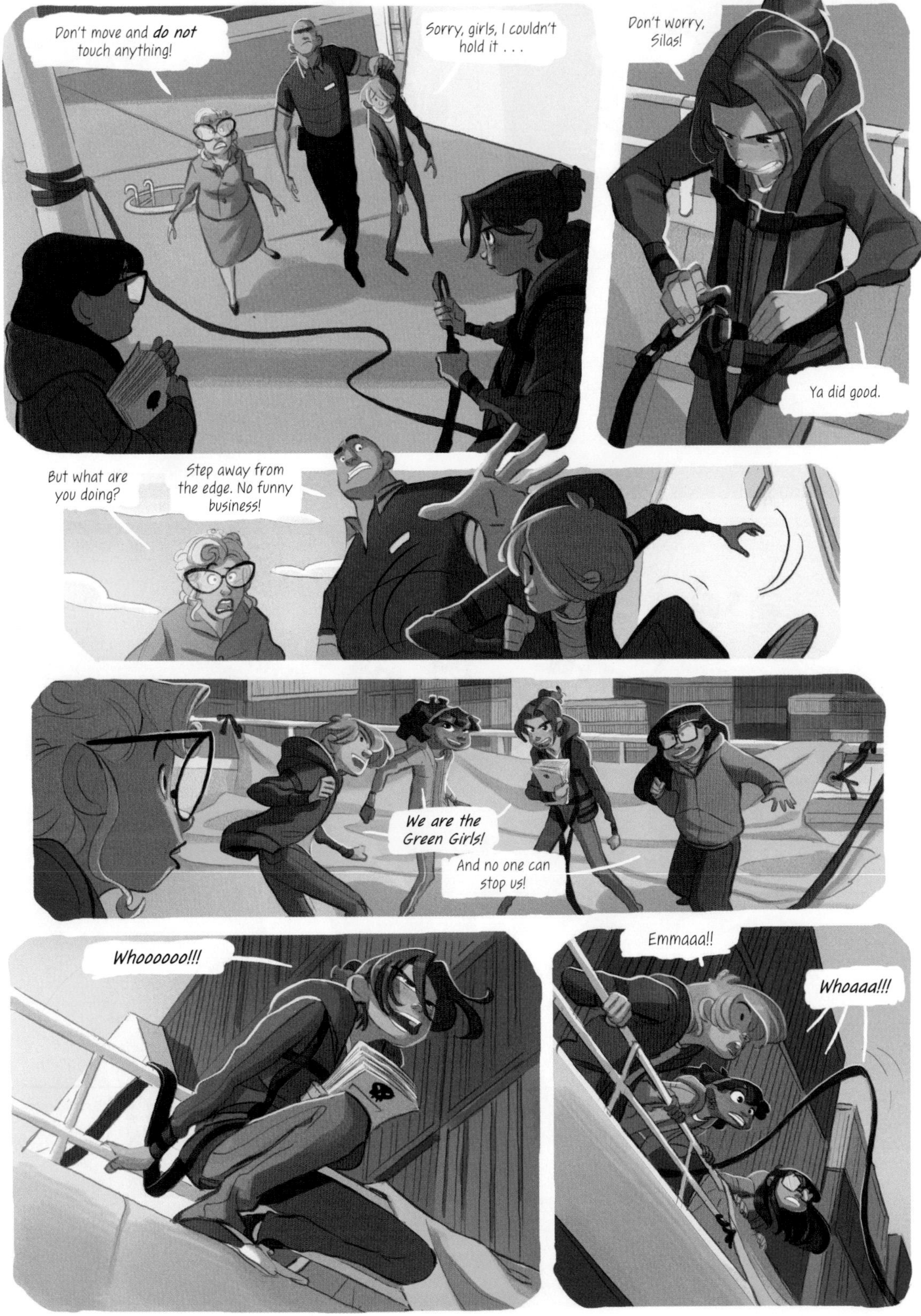
Don't move and **do not** touch anything!
Sorry, girls, I couldn't hold it . . .
Don't worry, Silas!
Ya did good.
But what are you doing?
Step away from the edge. No funny business!
We are the Green Girls!
And no one can stop us!
Whoooooo!!!
Emmaaa!!
Whoaaa!!!

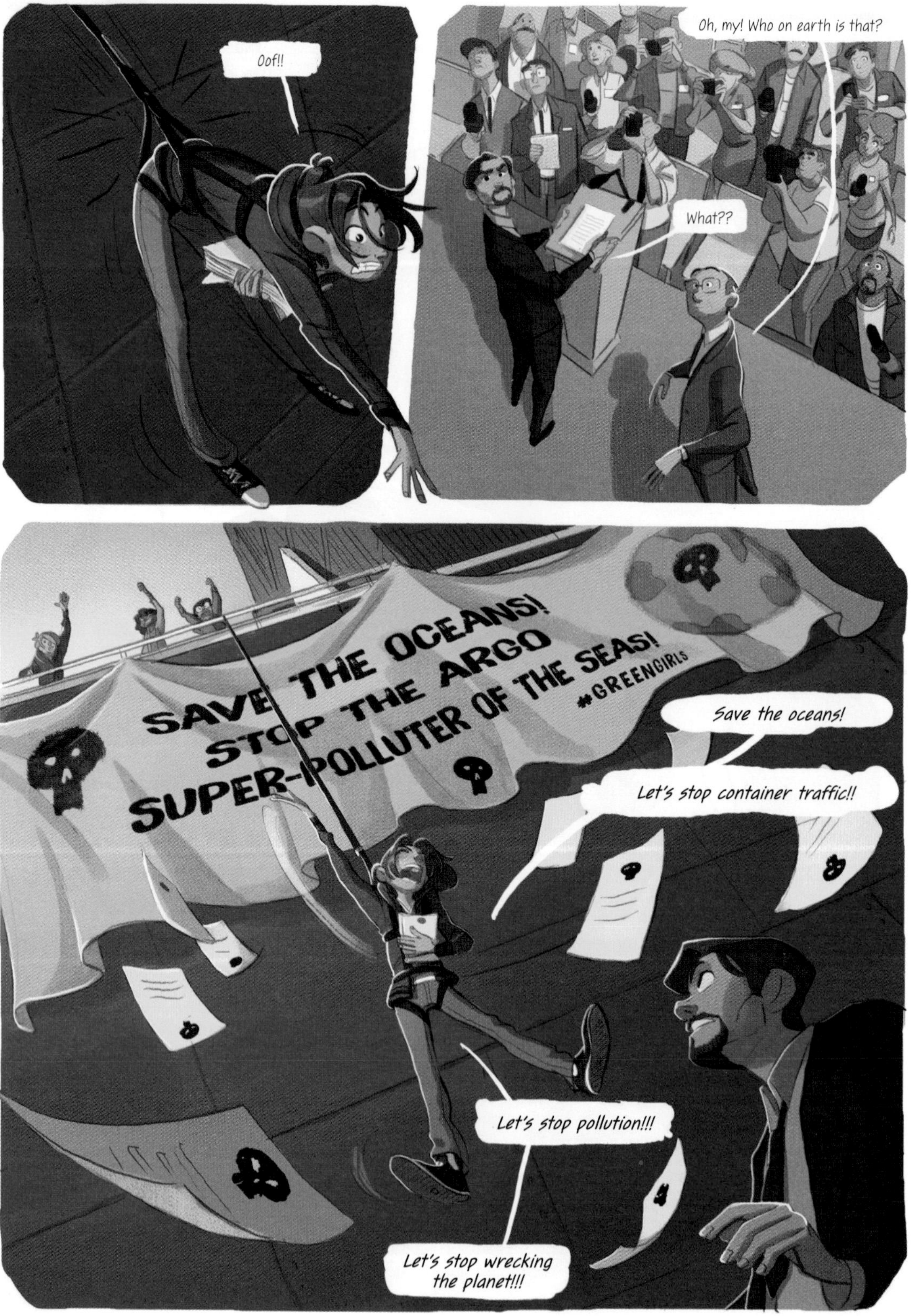
Oof!!
Oh, my! Who on earth is that?
What??
SAVE THE OCEANS!
STOP THE ARGO
SUPER-POLLUTER OF THE SEAS!
#GREENGIRLS
Save the oceans!
Let's stop container traffic!!
Let's stop pollution!!!
Let's stop wrecking the planet!!!

Emma???

Am I seeing things?

Hi Dad! What's up?

Since you couldn't pay me a visit . . .

I figured I'd come to you!

The terrorist up there is *your daughter?*

Get down from there right now!

What you're doing is dangerous!

No way! I'm not leaving!

Not until you promise to cancel the launch of this container ship.

Be serious, Emma!

I'm the minister of industry and trade.

Our economy **needs** boats like this . . .

No! You're wrong!

We don't need stuff made halfway across the world.

We don't need boats crossing the globe.

SAVE THE OCEA STOP THE AR SUPER-POLLUTER OF TH

We have a duty to **protect the planet!**

Who are the Green Girls?

THE OCEANS ARE DYING
STOP POLLUTING THEM!
#GREENGIRLS

No!

OK, Emma, I promise . . .

But come down from there.

I know what your promises are worth.

How many times have you skipped out on spending a weekend with me?

Huh? How many?

So I want you to swear in front of all these reporters . . .

You'll do everything, *everything*, to save our planet . . .

Because it's the only one we have!

Emma . . .

You know I can't . . .

Please, Dad!

Think about the future children of this planet . . .

And *your daughter!*

OK, my love.

66

My daughter is right. The Argo is a technological marvel . . .

But also the future biggest polluter of the ocean.

And now's the time to prevent that.

Wait a minute!

Yeaahhh!!!

We did it!!

OK, now are you coming down?

The minister misspoke. The Argo doesn't pollute . . . well, not really . . .

It'll pollute less with our new green fuel . . . eventually . . .

A little slack?

You got it!

No! Not that one!

SAVE THE OCEANS! STOP THE ARGO SUPER-POLLUTER OF THE SEAS!

Aaaahh!!

Emma!

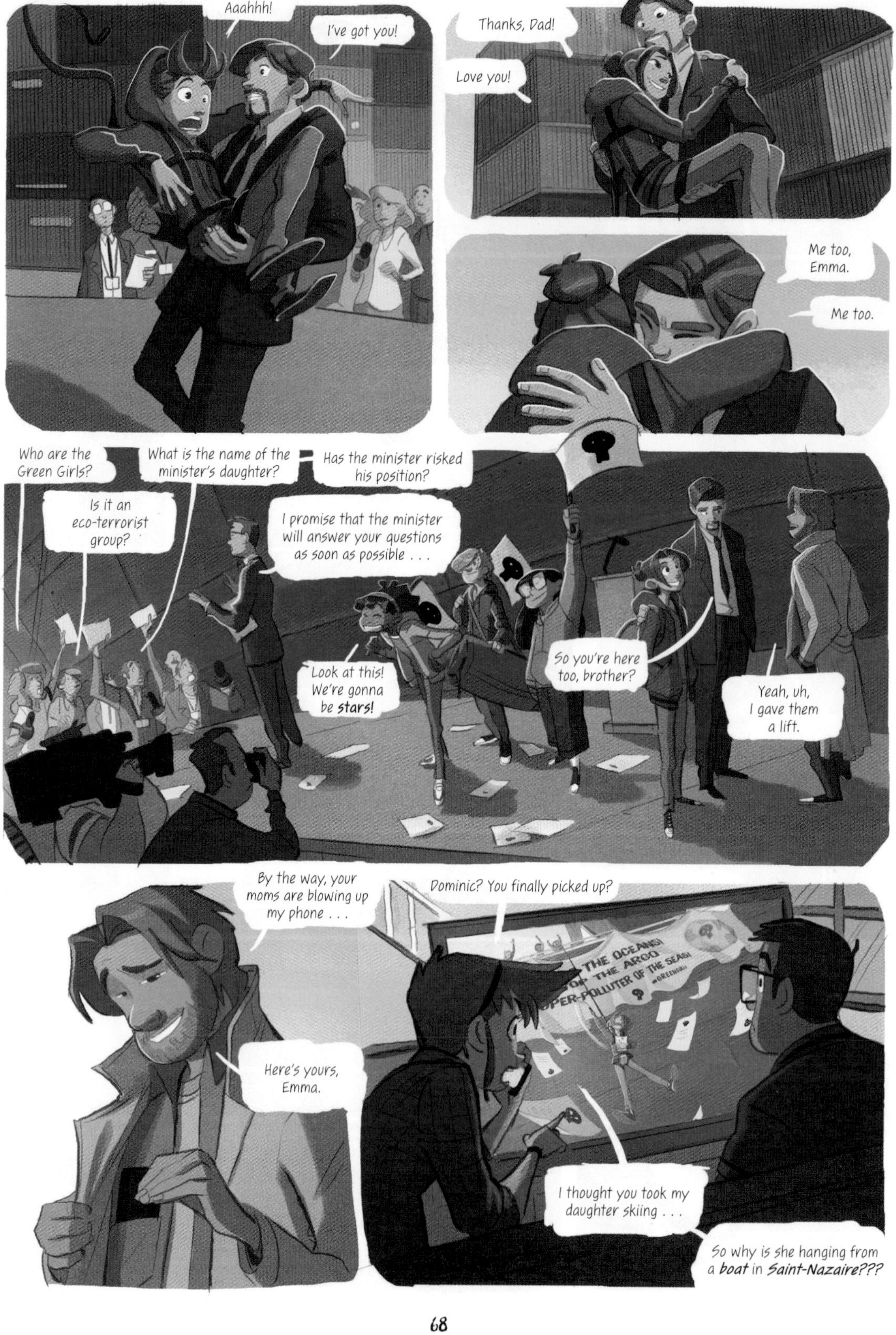
Aaahhh!
I've got you!
Thanks, Dad!
Love you!
Me too, Emma.
Me too.
Who are the Green Girls?
What is the name of the minister's daughter?
Has the minister risked his position?
Is it an eco-terrorist group?
I promise that the minister will answer your questions as soon as possible . . .
Look at this! We're gonna be **stars!**
So you're here too, brother?
Yeah, uh, I gave them a lift.
By the way, your moms are blowing up my phone . . .
Dominic? You finally picked up?
THE OCEANS!
OF THE ARGO
SUPER-POLLUTER OF THE SEAS!
Here's yours, Emma.
I thought you took my daughter skiing . . .
So why is she hanging from a ***boat*** in ***Saint-Nazaire???***

No TV! No internet!

And definitely no hangouts for three months!

But Mommm . . .

No! No "but Mom"!

You lied to me, you lied to your stepdad . . .

It's really not such a big . . .

I wanted to make a difference.

Don't even start!

Or I'll file kidnapping charges!!

OK, OK, OK!

It's not fair. Greta Thunberg's mom doesn't yell at her . . .

Well, Greta Thunberg doesn't sneak across the country!

And make Dad finally notice me.

Aww, my love.

Don't worry—your dad definitely noticed.

And with what he said, things will change, I'm sure.

You can't imagine how proud we are, Emma!

But no more lies.

You have to be a thirteen-year-old again . . .

OK, Mom.

69

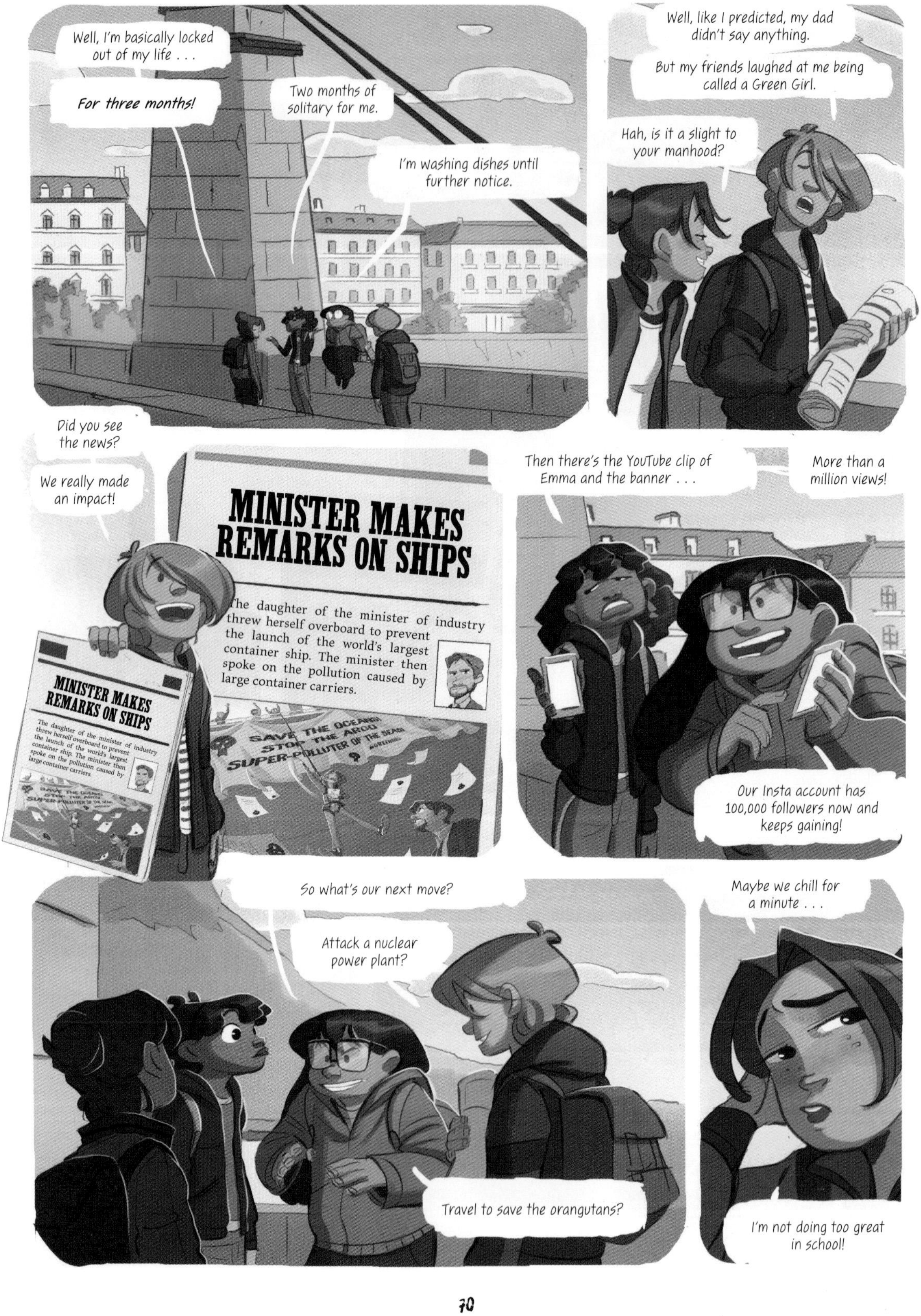

Well, I'm basically locked out of my life . . .
For three months!
Two months of solitary for me.
I'm washing dishes until further notice.
Well, like I predicted, my dad didn't say anything.
But my friends laughed at me being called a Green Girl.
Hah, is it a slight to your manhood?
Did you see the news?
We really made an impact!
MINISTER MAKES REMARKS ON SHIPS
The daughter of the minister of industry threw herself overboard to prevent the launch of the world's largest container ship. The minister then spoke on the pollution caused by large container carriers.
SAVE THE OCEANS! STOP THE ARCO SUPER-POLLUTER OF THE SEAS!
MINISTER MAKES REMARKS ON SHIPS
Then there's the YouTube clip of Emma and the banner . . .
More than a million views!
Our Insta account has 100,000 followers now and keeps gaining!
So what's our next move?
Attack a nuclear power plant?
Travel to save the orangutans?
Maybe we chill for a minute . . .
I'm not doing too great in school!

You all had so many questions that we thought it'd be a good idea to gather everyone together.

SAVE THE OCEANS! STOP THE ARGO SUPER-POLLUTER OF THE SEAS!

#GREENGIRLS

But first . . .

Let's talk to the activists!

Hi! Thanks for coming! I was asked to tell our story . . .

So I'll start at the beginning.

Three friends were tired of feeling useless . . .

And a guy wanted to do some good.

But actually, um . . .

I only have one thing to say!

No more talk!

Action!

And let's show everyone that even at thirteen . . .

We can change the world.

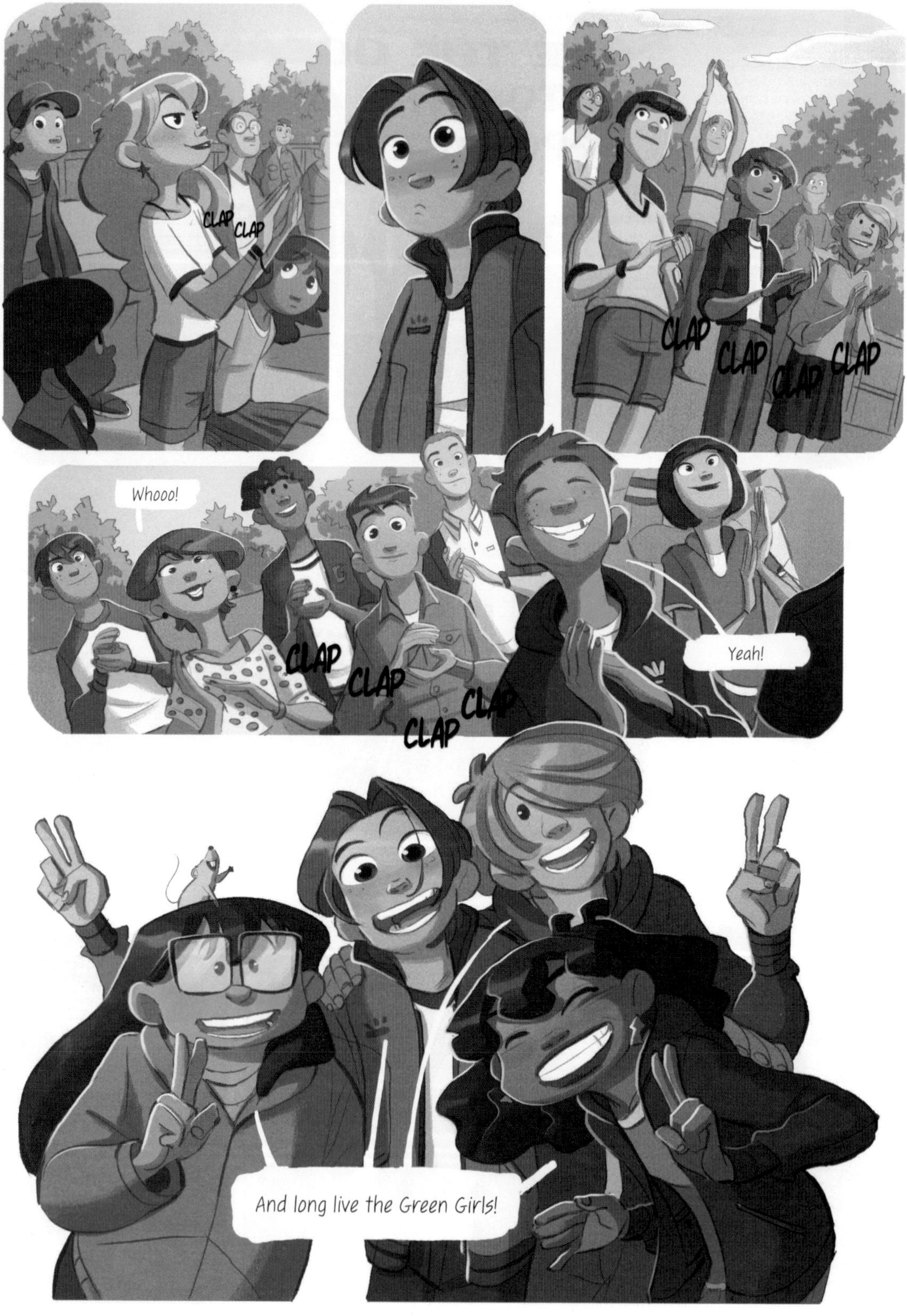
CLAP CLAP
CLAP
CLAP
CLAP
CLAP
Whooo!
CLAP
CLAP
CLAP
CLAP
Yeah!
And long live the Green Girls!

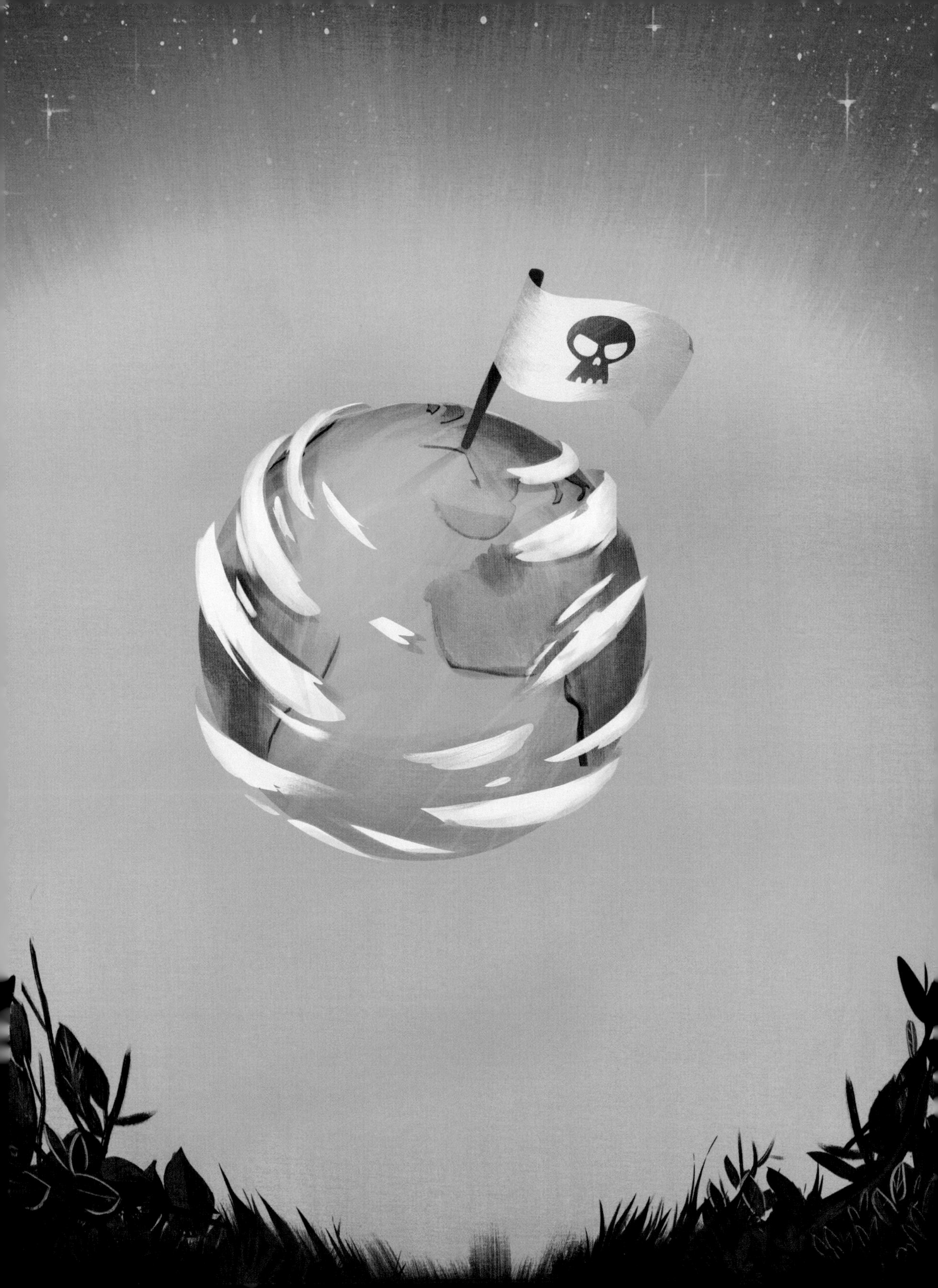

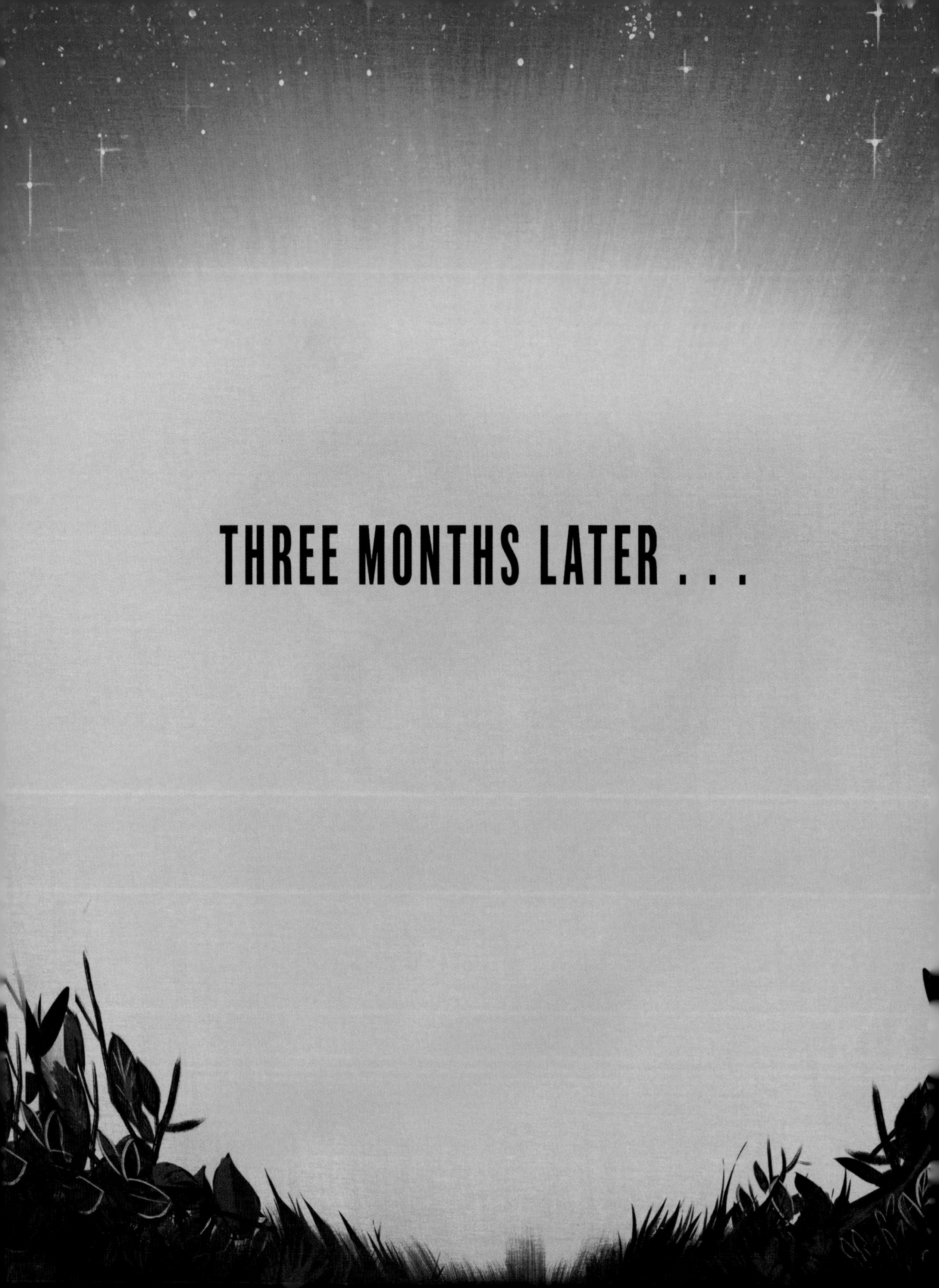
THREE MONTHS LATER . . .

You're late!

When we say 8:00 p.m., **we should stick to 8:00 p.m.!**

Not 8:30!

It's OK, Emma!

Our followers won't panic if our livestream is late.

It's the *principle.*

Fadila, you coming?

I'm—huff—doing—huff—my best.

Now, let's go over the plan!

We act fast and stay close . . .

But if we get spotted, we split up.

Don't forget to livestream while you're at it.

Huff . . . huff . . .

Perfect! Now the big question.

Who wants what color?

All right! The perfect place to stream.

Pssh! Insta live? That's **prehistoric.**

What if we did steps on TikTok? That would slap.

Are you gonna come up with the moves?

You're a dancer now?

Pssh! You don't have to be a dancer . . .

You just need the right beats!

Aren't there too many people around?

We'll get spotted!

That's what we **want,** Silas!

If you wanna get heard, you gotta knock loud.

OK, Emma, we're live . . .

Now!!

Hey everybody!

Welcome to a live action from the Green Girls.

Tonight's a first on the stream. We're tackling . . .

Electric scooters!

Not only are they parked everywhere, bothering pedestrians . . .

They're also **pollution machines!**

Their batteries are full of aluminum and lithium—and **very** difficult to recycle.

And their lifespan is super short: less than three years.

Not to mention the pollution when the batteries leak or get left in rivers.

Sorry, we're in the middle of a livestream—thanks!

So tonight, we'll show you how to stop these scooters from running . . .

With a little paint.

Here's the QR code that lets you rent the scooter.

A quick spray . . .

PSSSHHHHHTT

And it's impossible to borrow.

Couldn't be simpler.

Now—your turn!

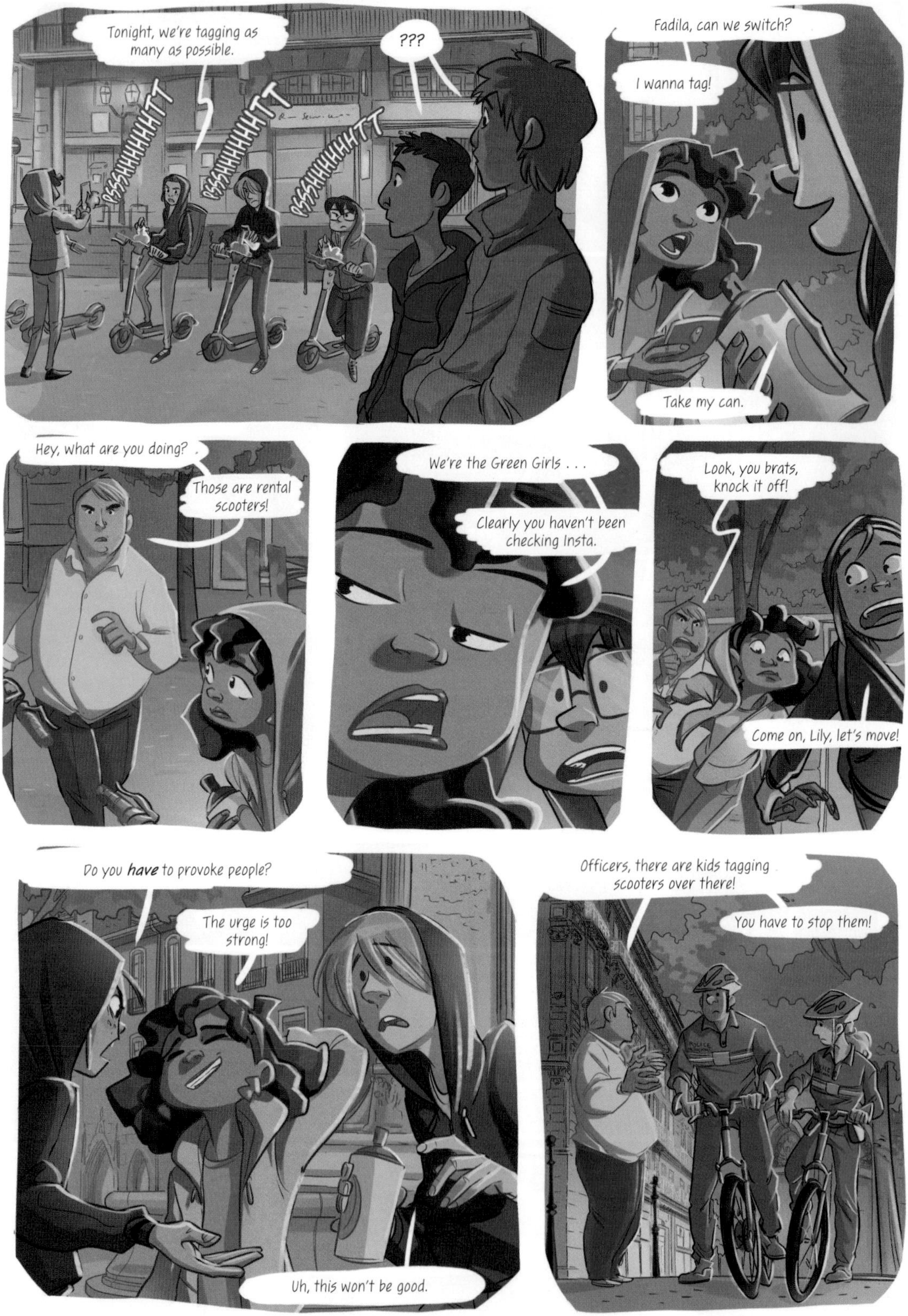
Tonight, we're tagging as many as possible.
PSSSHHHHHHTT
PSSSHHHHHHTT
PSSSHHHHHHTT
???
Fadila, can we switch?
I wanna tag!
Take my can.
Hey, what are you doing?
Those are rental scooters!
We're the Green Girls . . .
Clearly you haven't been checking Insta.
Look, you brats, knock it off!
Come on, Lily, let's move!
Do you **have** to provoke people?
The urge is too strong!
Uh, this won't be good.
Officers, there are kids tagging scooters over there!
You have to stop them!

Split up!!

Keep running, they're on our butts!

I feel so much *adrenaline!*

They're catching up!

Keep going! I know what to do.

Stoooooppp!!

!!!!

What are you doing out here this time of night?

And with cans of spray paint?

Me? Tagging scooters.

Uh, by myself.

That's it. You're coming with us to the station.

No. I'm thirteen.

You can't stop me!

You know there's a *juvenile* court.

Seriously? You'd put me in front of a judge for tagging?

Besides, you don't know who my father is.

So, you believe being the daughter of a politician . . .

Gives you the right to deface electric scooters?

JUDGE BARDY

Judge Bardy, thank you for giving me the chance to explain myself.

We're facing a global emergency . . .

And we have to do everything to stop climate change.

Those scooters consume tons of electricity, pollute when they're manufactured . . .

And pollute more if they're thrown away.

Never mind the accidents they cause!

These scooters, Judge, are a plague against which we must fight!!

JUDGE BARDY

I take your point, young lady . . .

And I even share your views.

But I'm here to enforce the law.

What you and your . . . *associates* did is vandalism.

And it can be punished by two years in prison and a 30,000 Euro fine.

For a thirteen-year-old kid?

Two years in prison?

Madame Judge, it's not that serious . . .

Calm down. I won't go that far.

Given that it's your first arrest.

And I know that you have good intentions.

But fighting for a just cause doesn't mean you can do **anything.**

And being thirteen doesn't mean you should get away with everything.

So, here's what I've decided . . .

As a result of acts of vandalism committed live on Instagram, at which she admits being present . . .

Emma Delaney, I'm giving you a warning . . . and requiring community service.

A warning?

Shh! Listen!

You will spend three Saturdays assisting an environmental organization.

And I would advise your friends who escaped the law to join you there.

But hear this, young lady!

I don't want to see you in here for vandalism ever again.

Is that clear?

JUDGE BARDY

You have my word, Judge.

Thank you, Judge.

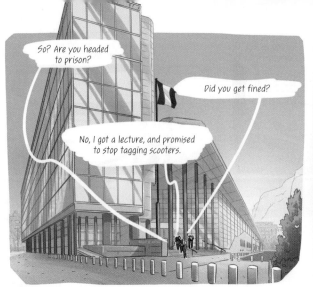

So? Are you headed to prison?

Did you get fined?

No, I got a lecture, and promised to stop tagging scooters.

I also have to volunteer somewhere.

The judge was kinda cool.

If that's the price to pay for getting our message out . . .

greer   We only got more likes on the Argo!

8k Liked

Booom! Blowing up the internet!

Just don't read the comments! People are so ignorant.

Emma, your father's here.

It's OK, Dad, it went really well.

I got a warning, nothing serious.

And you're proud of it??

I'm fed up with your nonsense, Emma.

My daughter, vandalizing scooters for social media hits . . .

You think that's good for my career?

It's not like we **broke** anything . . . Just covered some QR codes . . .

Since the Argo, I've tried to see you more often.

And this is how you thank me.

Stop being an irresponsible child . . .

And think about the consequences of your actions.

So? Did he offer you a job in the Ministry of Ecology?

He treated me just like an eight-year-old . . .

I bet he wishes I was behind bars instead.

Well, we asked for it. Getting yelled at is no surprise.

Oh yeah? No surprise?

And what did **your dad** say?

Oh, my dad doesn't notice anything.

He's always traveling, doing special effects for movies.

Wait, that's a cool job!

Yeah, **he's** having fun, but I never see him.

PALAIS DE JUSTICE

At least your dad's interested in what you do!

Our parents are all dumb . . . but we can't trade them.

Welcome to Clearer Rivers!

So which of you is Emma?

That's me, and these are my friends in the Green Girls.

Lily, Fadila, and Silas.

And Lady Mim!

What does your group do?

Lots of things—to improve the banks of the Isère and parts of the city.

We go to parks board meetings, city council meetings . . .

Really? Could we go ask the mayor to get rid of scooters?

And keep portable speakers with bad music off the streets?

And make downtown pedestrian-only?

And ban pet litter in the streets?

That's already banned!

Oh yeah? So why do I see it everywhere?

Those are all good ideas . . .

But I had something else in mind.

Oh yeah?

What do we get to do?

Picking up trash! I can't believe it!

This is our lowest moment.

I thought we were gonna do something *important*.

Not walk around in this muck.

It *is* pretty mucky.

Stop *complaining*, Lily!

We can't do something epic every day.

Change starts with small steps!

Don't you think it's pretty here?

It would be so nice to see it cleaned up!

Just look what's on the ground.

Fast food containers . . .

Used masks, safety gloves . . .

Even with trash cans everywhere!

At least some of it's biodegradable, right?

But it won't break down overnight.

Check this out. I picked it up before we left.

CLEARER RIVERS

PRESERVE OUR RIVERS!

Have you ever, without thinking about it, thrown a piece of trash into nature? This move will have an impact for months, even years, given the time it takes for your trash to break down in water.

Type of waste	Time to break down
Toilet paper	2 weeks
Cardboard	2 months
Tissue	3 months
Newspaper	3–12 months
Bus ticket	1 year
Chewing gum	5 years
Candy wrapper	5 years
Polystyrene container	80 years
Aluminum can	100 years
Plastic bag	450 years
Sanitary napkin	450 years
Disposable diaper	450 years
Surgical mask	450 years
Fishing net	600 years
Plastic bottle	1,000 years

So, next time, take a few seconds to throw your waste in a trash can. Nature and the rivers say thank you!

Five years? *For chewing gum!?*

I bet there are pieces under my desk older than that.

These masks are keeping us safe . . .

But now they get tossed everywhere too.

Man, 450 years!? That's long enough for our descendants to use.

Does that mean you're planning on having kids, Silas?

Um . . . yes . . . maybe . . .

Why, aren't you?

I'd need to find the dad first. Someone handsome, tall . . . and rich!

Oh. Uh. Right.

Or just someone who's cute when he blushes.

. . .

Are we interrupting?

Don't mind us!

Please, keep going!!

Now, should we drag this stuff back to HQ?

So, good haul?

Five bags in under two hours!

People are gross.

So that's what you do in this group?

Anything more exciting?

C'mon, we had fun.

You came at the right time!

We've planned an awareness campaign against palm oil.

To save the *orangutans???*

Amazing!!!

Oh no, you don't know what you've started.

Yes, orangutans and other species too.

We have fliers for supermarkets.

They're the biggest palm-oil sellers.

The flier explains it.

Nice!!

PALM OIL:
THE ORANGUTAN KILLER

Used by corporations at a mass scale because it is cheap to produce, the exploitation of palm oil is a true environmental disaster that should no longer be ignored.

A food revolution . . .

Palm oil was already in use during the time of the Pharaohs, then used in the 19th century as a mechanical lubricant or as an ingredient in pharmaceutical and cosmetic products. But only in the 20th century did it become essential in the food industry.

Easier to work with and less expensive than animal fats, and less harmful to health than hydrogenated vegetable oil, palm oil is utilized throughout the development of processed food products. Under the term "vegetable oil," it is found in many ready-to-eat meals, salty and sugary cookies, and all kinds of other products: chips, soups, spreads, baby formula, canned sardines, mayonnaise, tomato sauce, cereals, chocolate, grated cheese, crème fraîche, pastry, breads, and . . . ice cream! In fact, its use is so widespread that since 2006, palm oil production has doubled. Worldwide, 70 percent of imported palm oil is used in food, while actions by French consumer and environmental groups have reduced this figure to 50 percent in France.

. . . but an environmental disaster!

A palm bears fruit twice a month. The palm nut is transformed into oil by cold pressing, in oil mills close to the places of production, with very little labor. Which explains why this oil is so cheap.

Indonesia and Malaysia supply nearly 90 percent of the 70 million tons produced annually, which also come from countries such as Thailand, Nigeria, and Colombia. Faced with ever-increasing demand and the prospects of profit and employment opportunities, these countries may burn tropical forests to replace them with fields of palm trees. This releases into the atmosphere massive quantities of carbon that the forests originally captured in the ground. It also destroys sensitive ecosystems made of sometimes-irreplaceable plant and animal species. And the burnings may deprive local populations of their ancestral practices, often forcing them to work within the new palm-tree fields instead.

Orangutans threatened with extinction

Orangutans, a name that means "people of the forest," live only in tropical forests on the islands of Sumatra (Indonesia) and Borneo (Indonesia, Malaysia, and Brunei). When thousands of acres of these forests are sacrificed for the sake of palm plantations, the habitats and feeding grounds of these exceptional apes also get destroyed.

The three species of orangutans, the Bornean, Sumatran, and Tapanuli, are all categorized as "critically endangered." The Indonesian and Malaysian governments have created many nature reserves, but these territories only protect one-third of the orangutan populations. The rest of these animals live in forests threatened with destruction. Despite the work of many advocacy groups around the world, industrial and economic interests unfortunately remain a priority, to the detriment of the survival of these great apes.

Biofuel: a fake good idea

Biofuels are produced by replacing part of a fossil fuel with oil from biomass, such as oil-rich rapeseed, a part of the mustard or cabbage family. In other words, people replace a polluting and limited resource with a renewable one that can be produced in all countries. Simple and efficient.

But companies are obsessed with keeping production as cheap as possible. Even when it comes from the other side of the world, palm oil is more profitable than locally produced vegetable oils. This is why an old oil refinery near Marseille was converted into a palm oil refinery: since its opening, the Bioraffina factory has imported 550,000 tons, or 64 percent of what France consumes annually, with no intention of using the rapeseed produced by French farmers.

Following demonstrations by environmental groups and the grumbling of French rapeseed producers, plant manager J.J. Darrigol agreed to also process French vegetable oils and other residual oils, but palm oil remains the main oil refined in the plant. Moreover, a study commissioned by the European Commission shows that, if we consider the whole supply chain, greenhouse gas emissions from a biofuel based on palm oil are equivalent to three times those of fossil fuels. Three times!

Can we accept that we're sacrificing living beings on the other side of the world to make our cars run? No!!!

Let's say no to biofuels and products containing palm oil!

Let's be responsible for our consumption!
Let's be consum-activists!

CLEARER RIVERS

Oil in *ice cream?* That's wild.

Will a handout really change things?

I doubt it! My mom will always buy the same stuff for our family.

You gotta start somewhere.

If people reject products with palm oil . . .

Manufacturers won't use it anymore, and they won't need refineries for it.

And there's a refinery in France?

Yes, the one in the leaflet, Bioraffina.

A super-old one converted to increase profits.

Meet its chief executive, J.J. Darrigol.

He's your classic hypocrite.

Some have accused us of destroying forests on the other side of the world.

But they don't see the hundreds of families who thrive thanks to the jobs that our factories create each year!

Not to mention the delight people young and old derive from our products.

I assure you, there are only positives to our converting this factory.

Bioraffina. We're simply . . .

More refined.

All right. We're teaching him a lesson.

That orangutan killer!

That's it: our next action.

Location: the Bioraffina plant!

Yesssssss!!!

???

There are guided tours of the factory every day.

Easy! We get in there, spray-paint *Orangutan Killers* . . .

And we're outta there!

Or . . . we sabotage the whole factory! Put holes in their pipes . . .

And make a palm-oil geyser people can see for miles!

WHOOOOOOOSHHH!

And our follower count erupts too!

Have you all lost your minds!?!

Emma, did you already forget what the judge said?

If you see her again, she'll put you behind bars!

Calm down! You're so serious all of a sudden.

Obviously we're not blowing up the factory.

We're not?

But we *should* shame them on social media.

92

OK, so how do we get into this factory?

And how do we get permission from our parents?

We can't ask your uncle to cover for us again.

I might have an idea . . .

Next week, I've got climbing lessons.

And the course is in Cassis, right near Marseille.

If we all went there together, how's that for an excuse?

Climbing rocks. Fascinating.

Hold up, climbing is great!

Especially on real cliffs!

Fadila, didn't you say your dad didn't want you to take that class?

My mom said I could as long as . . .

I do the dishes for two months.

Two months? Yikes.

It's like you *already* got busted.

There's still one problem . . .

How do we get there?

I've taken a bus. But it's a long trip.

And I've already burned through my allowance for the month.

Leave it to me!

Now *I* have an idea . . .

Emma, it's reaaady!

I'm coming!

Tonight: farfalle carbonara.

Perfect! My stomach was about to digest itself.

With crème fraîche, of course.

This has been my signature dish since I was a student.

Never change a winning lineup.

Pssh! I can hear my Italian ancestors . . .

They're rolling over in their graves.

Hey, I wanna ask you something.

Fadila's doing a climbing course this weekend.

I'd love to go with her, but it's in Cassis.

Cassis? That's right near your mother's, isn't it?

Yes! Aubagne is a few miles away.

Yeah? Can we see Grandma Manon?

Well, it *will* be a three-day weekend . . .

And I haven't seen her in ages!

I'll be on call that weekend.

But you should have a girls' trip!

Emma, you'll surely want to go with your friends, right?

And if there aren't enough beds at Manon's, we'll camp out in the garden.

Could you take us all? That'd be great!

I remember tents in the garage.

Well, sounds like you've got everything planned already!

All right! I'll call Manon tomorrow.

Just promise me you won't tire her out. She just got out of the hospital.

Great!

I'll tell my friends . . .

Hollllld it!

First, we're trying my carbonara.

A little respect for my classic dish.

I'm not sure you can call this carbonara.

Crème fraîche or not, what matters . . .

Is a **mountain of parmesan!**

Yeah, yeah. Eat up before it gets cold!

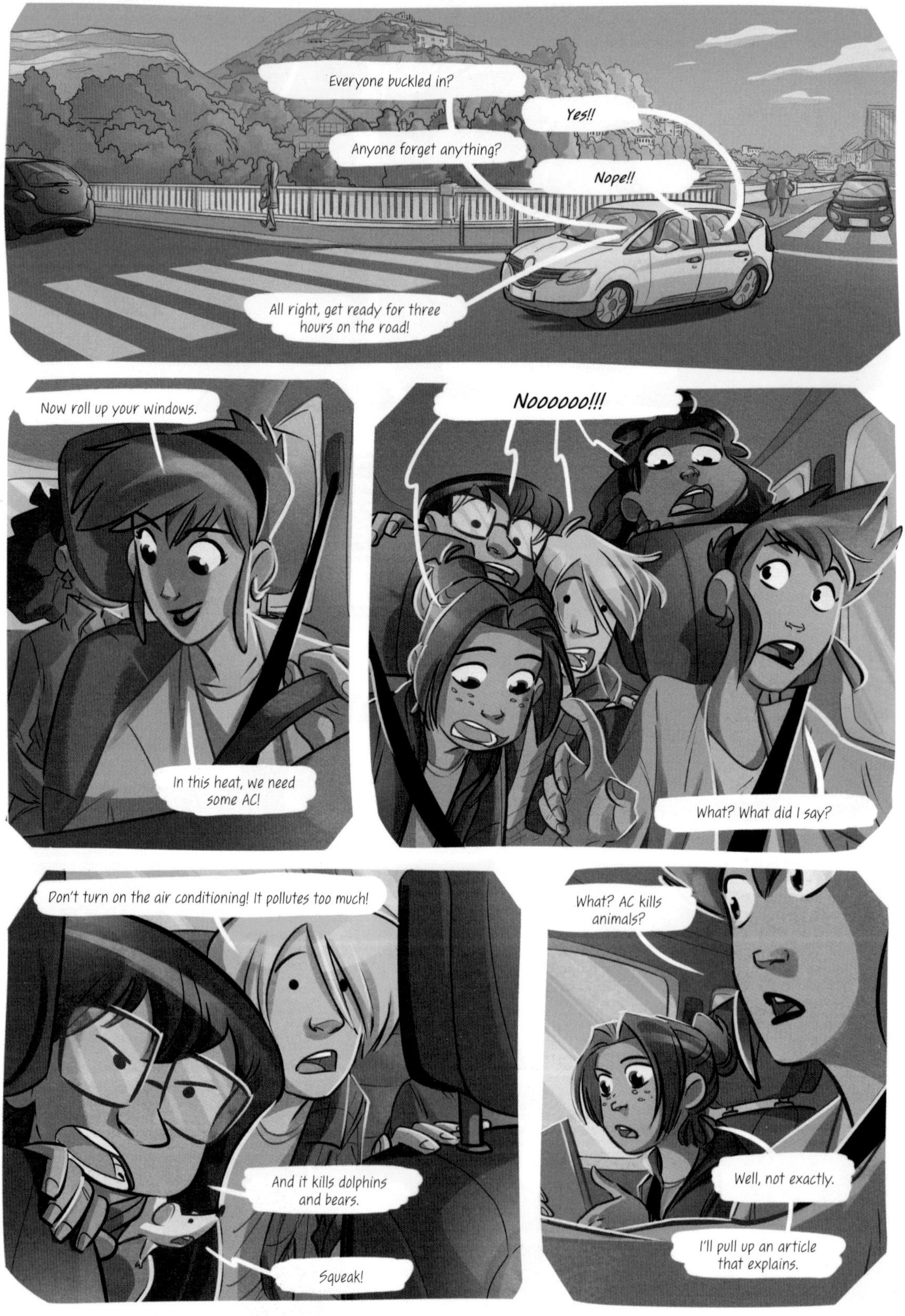
Everyone buckled in?
Yes!!
Anyone forget anything?
Nope!!
All right, get ready for three hours on the road!
Now roll up your windows.
In this heat, we need some AC!
Noooooo!!!
What? What did I say?
Don't turn on the air conditioning! It pollutes too much!
And it kills dolphins and bears.
Squeak!
What? AC kills animals?
Well, not exactly.
I'll pull up an article that explains.

AIR CONDITIONING: COMFORT—AT A COST TO THE ENVIRONMENT

It's crucial in places such as hospitals. But it has taken over our lives before a consideration of the consequences.

Greenhouse gases and more heat

Air conditioning functions in the same way as a refrigerator: an electric compressor compresses a refrigerant gas that produces cold and expels heat, thanks to the fan unit outside the dwellings. This poses two problems: if there is a leak in the system, the refrigerant gas can have a harmful environmental impact and attack the ozone layer (even if the recent gases are less harmful). And hot air, forced outside of buildings, contributes to an increase in urban temperatures—which leads to increased use of air conditioning. The phenomenon is accentuated in most cities, where concrete, a heat accumulator, has replaced green spaces, which better regulate the temperature and capture humidity.

Extreme heat and power outages

During periods of great heat, office buildings and shopping centers use high levels of air conditioning to maintain a pleasant temperature for their customers and employees, who expect to find comfort there. But this comes with consequences.

These consumption peaks coincide with periods when nuclear power plants, the main sources of electricity in France, have to operate slowly, because of the rise in the level of the rivers used to cool the nuclear towers.

Air conditioning in cars

To generate cold in a car, a compressor is activated by the running engine, and using air conditioning consumes between 10 and 20 percent more fuel. And in electric cars, some of the cold air generated must cool the batteries, which tend to heat up. But worst of all are drivers who leave their engines running while stopped to keep themselves cool, polluting the immediate surroundings with the exhaust gases. So, turn on the air conditioning or open the windows? Make the right choice!

Well, all right then! I won't put the AC on . . .

But let's open some windows!

That'll save gas too.

Nice breeze!

Better than a blow-dryer!

I think I swallowed a hair.

So your grandma's Manon? Classic. So French.

Oh, her real name's Simone.

I dunno why, but one day when I was little . . .

I called her Manon.

Now everyone calls her that.

I'm just asking you all to be careful.

She's 88 years old, and she just got out of the hospital.

She might be fragile.

Fadila will do the dishes for her. She loves to!

Excuse me?

We're here! Welcome to Aubagne.

What's that hill?

Garlaban!

Manon lives at the foot of it.

CLAC!

SNIIIIF

Hmm?

HOOONNK!!!

Manon!!

Oh, my granddaughter!

I'm so happy to see you!

99

This is one of my specialties. A true gift of the Pyrenees . . .

Piperade!

Oh, Manon, you're spoiling us!

What's in it?

Only the best: tomatoes, peppers, onions, eggs . . .

And for a Basque touch, Bayonne ham!

I'm getting full . . . but I want a little more!

Watch out, you won't be able to climb tomorrow!

Mmm! I didn't know something with this many vegetables could be so good.

Aren't you from Morocco?

Yes, I spent my childhood in Casablanca.

And with my husband and kids, we lived in Australia, Brittany, Touraine, and Provence.

But my heart's here, where my father was born!

I get that. My grandparents went back to Burkina Faso.

Manon, you're not about to tell them your whole life . . .

It's cool! Tell us some adventures . . .

You kids are adventurers yourselves!

What you did on that ocean liner, it reminded me of the old days.

Ha! We stirred things up.

Oh yeah?

Guess it runs in the family!

Bunch of **hotheads!**

It must have skipped a generation.

Come now, what about when we caught you skinny-dipping with your friends?

When your father turned on a yard light and saw bare butts around the yard?

You, Mom? **Really?**

Mom, you can't tell them that!!

Skinny-dipping?

Now you **have to** tell us . . .

Manon?

She's asleep! I'll get her to her room.

Will you kids clean up and pitch your tents?

Yes, Mom!

Yes, Emma's mom!

101

I . . . think we might be missing some parts.

I knew it! We should have done this in daylight.

But last summer we put it up in ten seconds!

You guys having trouble?

Everything's under control . . .

That wasn't **my** impression.

Check it out! This one's pitched.

VOOOOOOOOMMM

Whoooaaaaaaaaaa!!

You're lending us your tent? That's adorbs, Silas!!

What a gentleman!

We'll trade you ours!

I think I just got tricked.

Good night, kids!

I'll see you around eight.

Good night!!

OK, let's talk about tomorrow.

What's our **plan of action?**

Easy! We visit the factory . . .

Lose our tour guide . . .

And then tag everything with **"KILLERS"**!

Ah, that's basically what we did on the Argo.

Yeah, we need a new idea. But what?

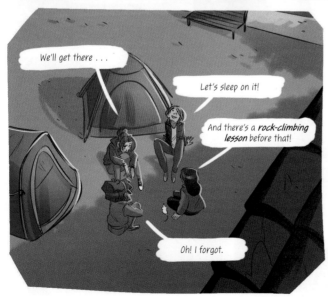

We'll get there . . .

Let's sleep on it!

And there's a **rock-climbing lesson** before that!

Oh! I forgot.

I don't know if I'm coming for that.

I don't see the point of crawling over rocks.

Hey everybody!

I'm Rodrigo. I'll be your climbing instructor.

It's my job to get you to the top of these cliffs!

We can't wait, Rodrigo!!

Careful, you might start *drooling*.

Now, the three most important things in climbing are . . .

Safety, safety . . .

And safety!

Ha ha ha ha ha!!

To start, I'll check your equipment.

Who wants to go first?

Oh, me! Me!

You *sure*, Lily?

Has she climbed anything other than a fence?

Perfect!

Ready to lead the way?

Oh, uh, no problem! I'm not afraid . . .

I'm afraaaaaaiiiiid!

Come get meeeeeeeeeee!!

Come on, Lily, this part's easy!

I'm gonna dieeee!!!

No, Lily, you've just frozen up!

There's a place to grab on your right!

She is *so* annoying.

I thought she had experience!

You shouldn't believe everything Lily says.

I can't move.

Calm down! Listen closely to me.

Just shift your arm! There's a handhold . . .

There you go, Lily!

When you think everything's going wrong, remember to keep calm.

The solution's usually right at hand.

I'll remember that.

No one's leaving me alone on a cliff again, OK!?!

Pshh, you weren't alone . . .

And you had a rope securing you!

But the next time someone asks you if you've done any climbing . . .

Just say *no!*

All right, all right . . .

Even if that someone is super handsome.

Even if your heart starts to flutter!

All right, I'm good!

You too? Rodrigo, um, super handsome?

Uh, obviously!

But not *cute.*

Anyway, planning time! Who has the cans?

I've got five in the false bottom of my bag.

Same!

And I have pliers and stuff for opening gates and breaking padlocks.

Get ready, Bioraffina.

The Green Girls are coming!

106

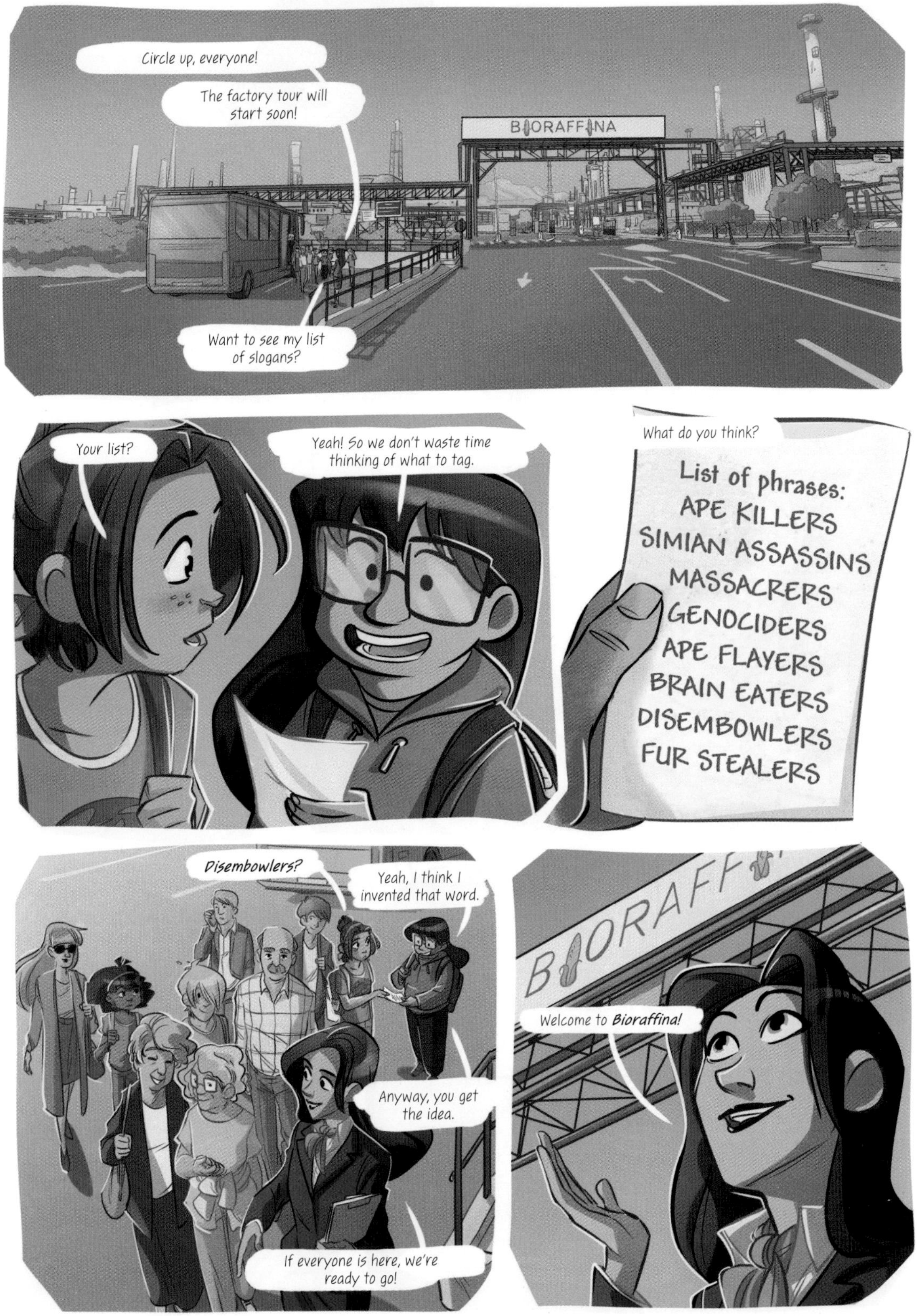

Circle up, everyone!
The factory tour will start soon!
BIORAFFINA
Want to see my list of slogans?
Your list?
Yeah! So we don't waste time thinking of what to tag.
What do you think?
List of phrases:
APE KILLERS
SIMIAN ASSASSINS
MASSACRERS
GENOCIDERS
APE FLAYERS
BRAIN EATERS
DISEMBOWLERS
FUR STEALERS
Disembowlers?
Yeah, I think I invented that word.
Anyway, you get the idea.
If everyone is here, we're ready to go!
BIORAFF
Welcome to *Bioraffina!*

Before you enter our factory . . .

There's a simple formality at the security office.

Security? Already?

Nothing to worry about.

They don't have a right to search us.

And we put stuff in the false bottoms anyway.

Hello. May I see your ID?

Huh?

This site has classified areas.

So I have to record the name of each visitor.

Oh, sure, here you go!

And now you get a *badge!!*

Looks sharp, right??

B O RAFFINA

Oh, uh, very!

Thanks!

You can follow the group now.

Enjoy your trip!

B O RAFFINA

Hello. May I see your ID?

Can I see that list?

Welcome to the heart of a technological marvel!

The first refinery in France devoted to the production of biofuels.

A former oil refinery, completely redesigned for the needs of the modern world.

Excuse me, I have a question.

Why do you say "biofuel"?

It's not organic, right?

Great question!

In fact, it's unrelated to organic farming.

But our fuels are made from organic materials known as biomass . . .

Instead of fossil fuels!

Here, you'll only find palm oil or rapeseed!

Nothing polluting the environment.

Our next stop: *the factory control center!*

How long do we have to listen to this?

Tell them they're killing animals!

We need the right moment to slip away . . .

Gotta say, the factory *is* super 'grammable.

Click!

You've got to be kidding.

What, you don't see it?

This is the factory's main building.

Don't get lost in the hallways!

This is the perfect moment—go!!

Nice! No one saw us.

We don't have much time now.

Listen up!

Let's all head in one direction . . .

And tag as much as possible.

And get a pic each time for Instagram!

They'll die of shame!

Unbelievable!

???

Stay right there, please.

In a factory, accidents can happen in a flash.

Careful, we're minors!

And we're recording everything . . .

Our followers will see it live!

SECURITY

CRRRACK!

That's why you're kindly gonna give us your phones.

Or we'll have to take them by force.

OK, OK, no need to get rough!

Ah, jeez . . .

What are you going to do to us??

To you, nothing.

But someone wants to talk . . .

. . . to your leader!

Me??

SAVE OUR EARTH

Hello, Miss Delaney.

You don't have the right to sequester me!!

And how do you know my name?

Sequester! Now *that's* a big word.

And your name's on the list at reception.

We've been aware of your little group since the Argo.

Hey, you're Darrigol!

The orangutan killer!

We came to teach you a lesson.

Oh, is that who I am?

Orangutans, rhinos, tigers. Polar bears, obviously.

I'm truly heartless. Ha ha!

Now, instead of calling the police and embarrassing your father . . .

I want to give you a chance to see who we truly are.

I already know!

You're killers, destroying forests!

You only see one side of the coin.

Let me show you what's on the back.

Don't just look at this factory. Look beyond it!

Homes for our employees. Schools. Stadiums. Restaurants. Shops . . .

We helped build a city. Helped families live in comfort.

The whole local economy depends on this plant.

Not to mention the biofuels we produce, making society healthier.

And on the other side of the planet, you're destroying whole forests.

Animals' natural habitats.

And the farmers there with better lives thanks to these projects?

Or the French farmers whose rapeseed we process in this factory?

What do you think?

Uh . . .

And what are you gonna do with us?

Nothing. I'll leave you to reflect on your actions.

But if you're found around here again, retribution will be swift.

And here's a tip for your next supersecret operation.

Don't livestream it on Twitch!

113

Oof, that was close.

All they did was confiscate our paint.

Thanks *a lot*, Lily, by the way.

Me? I didn't do anything!

You weren't the one who started streaming on Twitch??

No, actually, I **wasn't!**

Don't make **me** your scapegoat!

Stop, you two! I was the one who went live.

See? **Wasn't** me who messed up.

But why'd you do that?

I wanted to put these animal killers on blast.

And I knew a livestream would get people's attention . . .

I just wanted to help.

Well, it did mess up the plan . . .

But maybe it wasn't the **best** plan . . .

I'll do better, promise.

BIORAFFIN

Look, the tour's over.

The bus'll be here soon . . .

I can't wait to go home . . .

I'm so embarrassed.

Do we find another action?

You're discouraged already, Emma?

What do you want to do? Go back?

They'll spot us the second we get close.

Maybe, but Bioraffina's the perfect target!

They're animal killers! Forest destroyers!

Monsters!

We should still make a video for Insta.

Maybe say the factory has a dangerous leak . . .

Yeah, uh, and they're covering up the scandal!

Wait, no, we're not inventing anything!

We don't lie to our followers.

Well, we can't *give up.*

We'll bounce back!

Yeah. When you think everything is screwed up . . .

The solution's usually right in front of you.

Yeah . . .

I wish it were that easy.

Dinner's ready!

Comiiing!!

Manon's not eating with us?

She's resting in her room.

Her treatment makes her really tired.

So how was the first day of climbing?

PSSSCHHHHTTT !!

Ha ha! Got you, mosquito!

You're not getting *my* blood!

Out here, the wind blows that spray away as soon as it leaves the can.

I guess AC on the terrace is out of the question.

We've got citronella candles and flypaper . . .

What is the **point** of mosquitoes!?

Why can't we just get **rid** of them??

Be careful what you wish for.

Ever heard of mosquito control campaigns?

MOSQUITO CONTROL: NECESSARY EVIL OR ENVIRONMENTAL DISASTER?

Ever wanted to get rid of mosquitoes? Well, the cure could be worse than the disease.

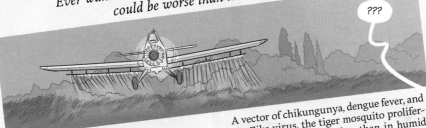

Searching for a solution

In infested areas, the mosquito is a real scourge. This insect is a vector for the spread of diseases in tropical areas, as well as a nuisance in temperate regions. In areas such as Europe's Rhône delta, a bio-insecticide, BTI, was used in the mid-2000s as a response. Reputed to only attack biting mosquitoes and thus preserve the ecosystem, studies have shown that non-biting mosquitoes were also affected, depriving their predators (spiders, dragonflies, swallows) of food and therefore impacting the entire food chain. These studies have also shown that BTI has residual effects, including repercussions several years after its spraying, threatening the ecosystem in the long term.

A new threat: the tiger mosquito

The tiger mosquito came from Southeast Asia and arrived in Europe in the 1980s thanks to international trade. This breed of mosquito, active during the day and very voracious, is progressing throughout France, with no natural predator slowing down its spread.

A vector of chikungunya, dengue fever, and the Zika virus, the tiger mosquito proliferates in urban areas, rather than in humid areas, which is part of why it is difficult to eradicate. Some regions have had to take quick action. Solutions have involved the use of a very toxic chemical insecticide: deltamethrin. It is effective on adult mosquitoes, attacking the nervous system of the insects, but harmful for biodiversity, especially for bees (increasing their mortality rates) but also for humans (increasing the risk of hyperactivity in children).

Many experiments have been done to protect urban areas, such as machines that attract mosquitoes with CO_2, coupled with vacuum cleaners that trap insects. No solution is perfect yet. For now, to respect nature, maybe we just have to put up with the mosquito!

Point taken!

I had no idea tiger mosquitos attacked during the day.

And it doesn't just take advantage of international travel . . .

We're seeing it spread across France more and more.

That's one of the downsides to globalization.

It's wild how human activity is changing the planet.

Everything's moving around, and we can't control it.

Like the coronavirus!

Or Pokémon.

But there's an easy solution to mosquitoes.

Their own wildlife sanctuaries!

Perfect! Problem solved.

Maybe bring by school tours, so they can snack a little . . .

Sanctuaries?

For mosquitoes?

Just kidding!

Ha ha ha ha!

You guys are so dumb.

And I knew you were joking!!

Room service!

Here's dinner, Manon.

Come in, granddaughter!

You have a TV in your bedroom?

Yes. I have trouble walking to the living room.

But at night, I only listen to the radio.

Oh, that looks good . . . even if your mother cooked.

I always tried to give her tips, but she never listened!

It's true! Even using your recipes . . .

Nothing compares to your cooking.

Now what's the matter, dear?

You have sadness in your eyes.

Nothing gets by you, Manon.

It wasn't a great day.

Tell Grandma all about it.

Well, we found a new, uh, project for the Green Girls . . .

But they're too big.

We just can't get at them.

Let me tell you a story.

When I was younger, in the scouts, we had a leader who humiliated the kids.

No one dared say anything. He was very commanding, with a spotless reputation.

But I couldn't bear to see my friends crying. We had to do something!

So I hatched a plan.

Tell me!!

I was in charge of the end-of-year show . . .

So I wrote a play about all the bad things he'd done.

And I played his role myself, in front of all the parents.

Without me saying so, everyone understood who I was aiming for.

He was so ashamed, he didn't dare mock anyone else.

Whoa! How did you know it would work?

Because, with some people, their image is the most important thing.

And that's where you have to get at them.

Thanks for the advice, Manon!!

Above all, don't get discouraged.

With any problem, there's a solution.

Otherwise, there's no problem!

That's what we have to do! Shame him in front of everybody!

Yeah! But we don't have to put on a play, right?

What about a flash mob?

Those are totally over.

What we need is attention from journalists . . .

But I don't know how!

You should call them and say the factory has a leak!

Or a *big explosion* seen from miles away!

I know someone who could fake something like that . . . and he doesn't live too far!

Yeah, but once journalists get there, what do we actually do?

I know . . .

But we'll need some climbing gear.

Should we ask Lily to bat her eyes at Rodrigo?

That's the *real* question . . .

Can she talk to the handsome instructor without fainting?

Ha ha ha ha!

All right, all right . . .

Am I getting roasted tonight or something?

Well, we still have a ways to go . . .

Then we'll arrive at one of the most beautiful views in the area.

What are we going to learn . . . huff . . . today?

The very best part of climbing . . .

Rappelling!

It's so beautiful!

This place is perfect—like humans still haven't messed it up.

I really wish that were true.

You can count on people to always make a mess.

But isn't this a natural park?

Like a sanctuary, right?

Yeah, a protected area. But only since 2012.

For decades, the site was polluted by red sludge from factories in Gardanne and elsewhere.

Look at this. It explains everything.

THE CALANQUES RED MUD SCANDAL

In 2012, France's Calanques National Park was created, protecting the coastline between Marseille and Cassis. But despite this, industries continue to dump their red sludge offshore. We haven't seen the end to this scandal yet!

Fifty years of pollution!

Produced during the manufacturing of alumina and aluminum, red mud contains heavy metals including lead, mercury, and chromium. Normally, before storage, it is dried in vast basins. An exception is a factory in Gardanne which obtained, in 1966, the right to expel this sludge off the coast of Cassis, thanks to a 29-mile (47-kilometer) pipeline between the factory and the underwater canyon of Cassidaigne. This same canyon rests only a few hundred meters from one of the richest marine ecosystems on the French Mediterranean coast.

In half a century, more than 20 million tons of harmful manufacturing residue, containing mercury and arsenic, has been dumped, with certain consequences for the area's marine ecosystem.

The difficult creation of the park

From the beginning of the 20th century, the area's inhabitants have wanted to protect this magnificent place and maintain its fragile balance. Over time, people saw the need to create a national park, in order to prevent urban, industrial, or railway projects that would cause further harm. But it was far from easy . . .

Several years and hundreds of meetings were necessary before the area received the designation of national park in 2012. The Calanques National Park encompasses the area's creeks, its coast, and the islands along the coast as well as more than 100,000 acres on the sea.

Everyone thought that this development would put an end to pollution from red mud. . . . But the Gardanne plant retained the right to dump its sludge on the site.

An endless fight

In 2015, a new hope arose: the authorization period for discharging waste into the sea was about to expire, and many people hoped that this environmental disgrace was coming to an end. Many environmental protection groups stepped up to the plate, supported by the minister of ecology at the time. . . . But all hopes were dashed when the prefecture extended this right to pollute for six additional years.

The plant was required to have been brought up to new standards in 2021, reducing the harmfulness of its waste discharge. However, another step remains: requiring that it no longer deposit sludge in the sea.

And there's another challenge: a typical industrial solution would be to dry the waste on land, which could pollute groundwater. Is that solution even worse?

That's wild! *Unbelievable!*

It's been going on for decades . . . and nobody does anything?

We thought the polluters would stop when the park was created, but we were wrong!

It's hard to fight against big business.

Even the minister of ecology of the time said he was helpless.

That's politicians for you!

A bunch of do-nothing . . .

I *hope* you don't mean my dad!

Wait! Uh, no! I didn't . . .

Somebody should think before speaking.

The important thing is that it will be harder to defile this magnificent place . . .

It's so scenic!!

AAAAAAAHHHHHHHHH!!!

Wheeeeeeeee! That was great!

Can I go again?

Well done! Nice drop.

But you'll have to wait till tomorrow.

Is that the same girl who was crying for her mom yesterday?

Weird, huh?

She always amazes me.

Hey, uh, can we keep the harnesses for the night?

To practice putting them on?

Uh . . . sure, why not . . .

Just remember to bring 'em back!

Hey!! Down there!

Am I good to go??

Yeah! You got this, Silas!

BEEEP
BEEEEEEEP

Now rest up! Tomorrow we're going to the biggest rock wall around.

???

Who's *that?*

What's up, kids?

Want to cause a ruckus?

Piero!!

Thanks for coming!

Hey big guy!

I'm always up for a bit of trouble.

This is Piero, my godfather!

He's the guy who's going to help us out.

I was able to get your costumes and fireworks.

But I don't *totally* get what you're going for . . .

It's OK, we'll explain . . .

Everything's coming together—except for one thing.

Our choreography!

Sure, but we can make it up.

Yeah, that part's easy!

Just leave the steps to me!

You'll see, girls . . .

We're gonna be the queens of TikTok!

Are you going to bed already?

Yeah, we're all beat!

I'll just say good night to Manon.

KNOCK
KNOCK
KNOCK

It's Emma.

Hello, my dear!

Come on in!

Grandma attack!!!

Ha ha, easy, kiddo!

How'd everything go today?

We took your advice!

We've found a way to embarrass the big boss.

Well done! You're really growing up . . .

I'm proud of you.

Now give me a hug!

I love you, Manon!

You too, Emma.

3:30 a.m.!? *Seriously??*

Can't we wait *a little?*

No time to waste, Lily.

Let's go! Piero's at the gate.

Just gotta prop Lily up and we're there.

C'mon kids, no lounging around!

The sunrise won't wait for us.

Sorry we're dragging a bit . . .

I'm just not a morning person.

Especially when it's the middle of the night.

Sure, sure . . . We ready?

Well, that's the plan!

Risky, huh? I like it!

Unless the security guards spot us . . .

Yeah, it'll have to be really discrete.

May the force be with us . . .

Look at *that* . . .

128

Whoa!!

We might not like the place . . .

But the refinery looks pretty beautiful at night.

Remember, 5:00 a.m. sharp! No earlier!

Don't worry!

How heavy are these costumes??

Now, time to get dressed.

Wish we could turn on a light . . .

Don't! They'll see us!

Hey, what did you put on first . . .

The costume or the harness?

All right, only five seconds!

4 . . . 3 . . . 2 . . .

One!

05:00

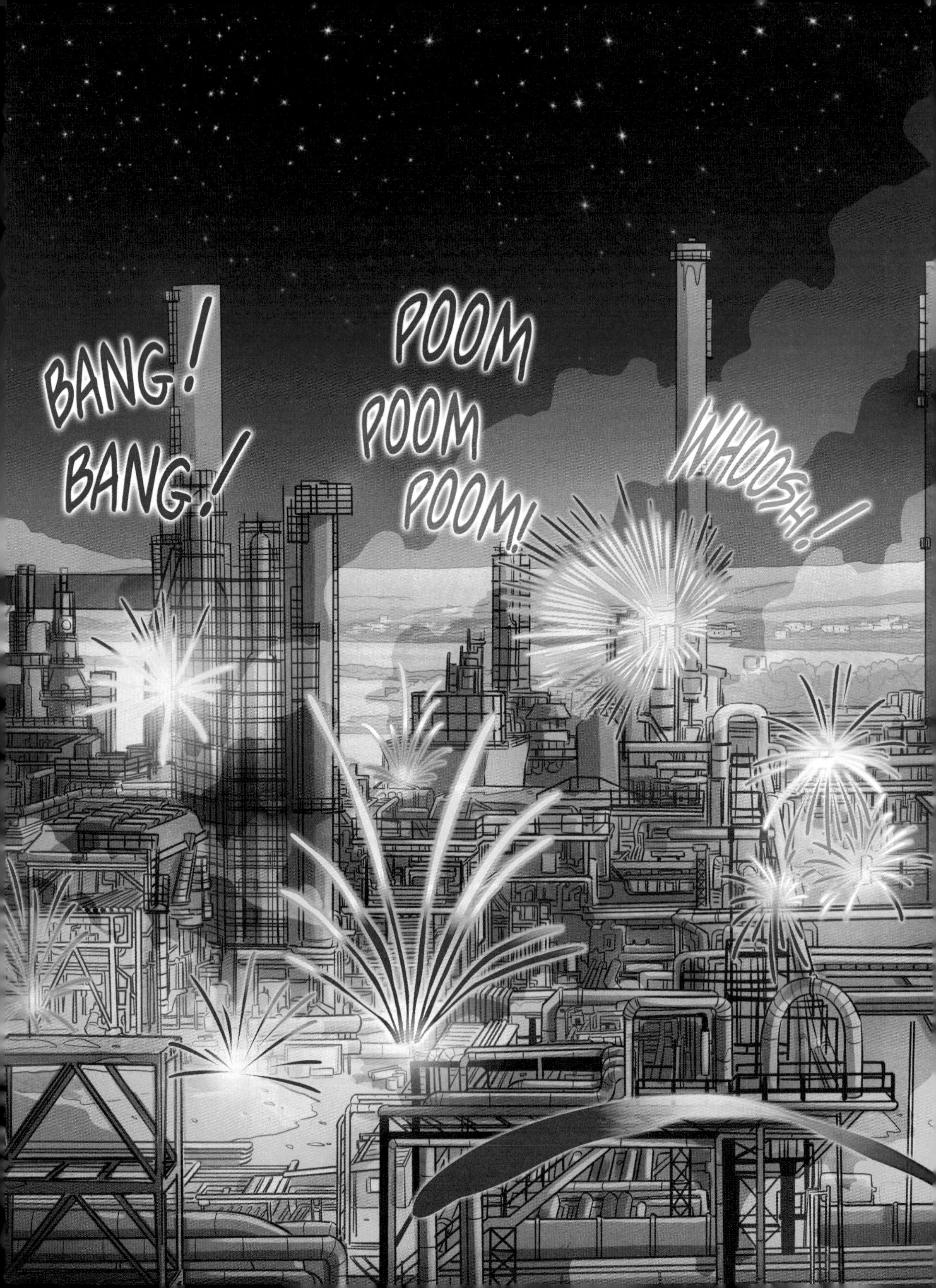
BANG!
BANG!
POOM
POOM
POOM!
WHOOSH!

Intense!

If I lived around here, I'd be bugging out!!

That's the goal, right?

Like my godfather's work?

He's one of the best in the business!

Oh yeah!

Time for part two!

I'll send some journalists a clip, and you call for help!

Yeah, loud noises at the refinery . . .

Big, bright lights, and a booming sound!

My kids are scared! It could be *dangerous!*

The press is coming . . .

Now for part three!

Let's climb!

Do it fast . . .

Does everyone remember the steps?

I found some great music . . .

We good?

131

Grrooaaannn??

Yes? Do you know what time it is!?

Sorry boss, it's an emergency.

There might've been an explosion!

Whaaat???

Where's the damage? Was it an attack?

That's what's weird. Everything seems fine!

Looks like it was just some fireworks.

Only noise and flashing lights.

What could this mean?

Saboteurs who do no damage?

Sir! Sir!

The media's at the entrance.

Should we send them away?

No, I'll speak with them.

There's no bad publicity . . .

What are those booming noises?

Is there danger nearby?

Members of the press, I assure you nothing serious has happened.

Our technicians have inspected the grounds, and despite the commotion . . .

Our facilities have not been damaged.

We assume it's pranksters playing with firecrackers.

Why would they do that?

Apart from scaring local residents?

We don't know yet.

But we'll find out who's to blame!

Maybe they're behind you.

Behind me . . . ?

I don't believe it.

Remember the moves!

One, two, three . . .

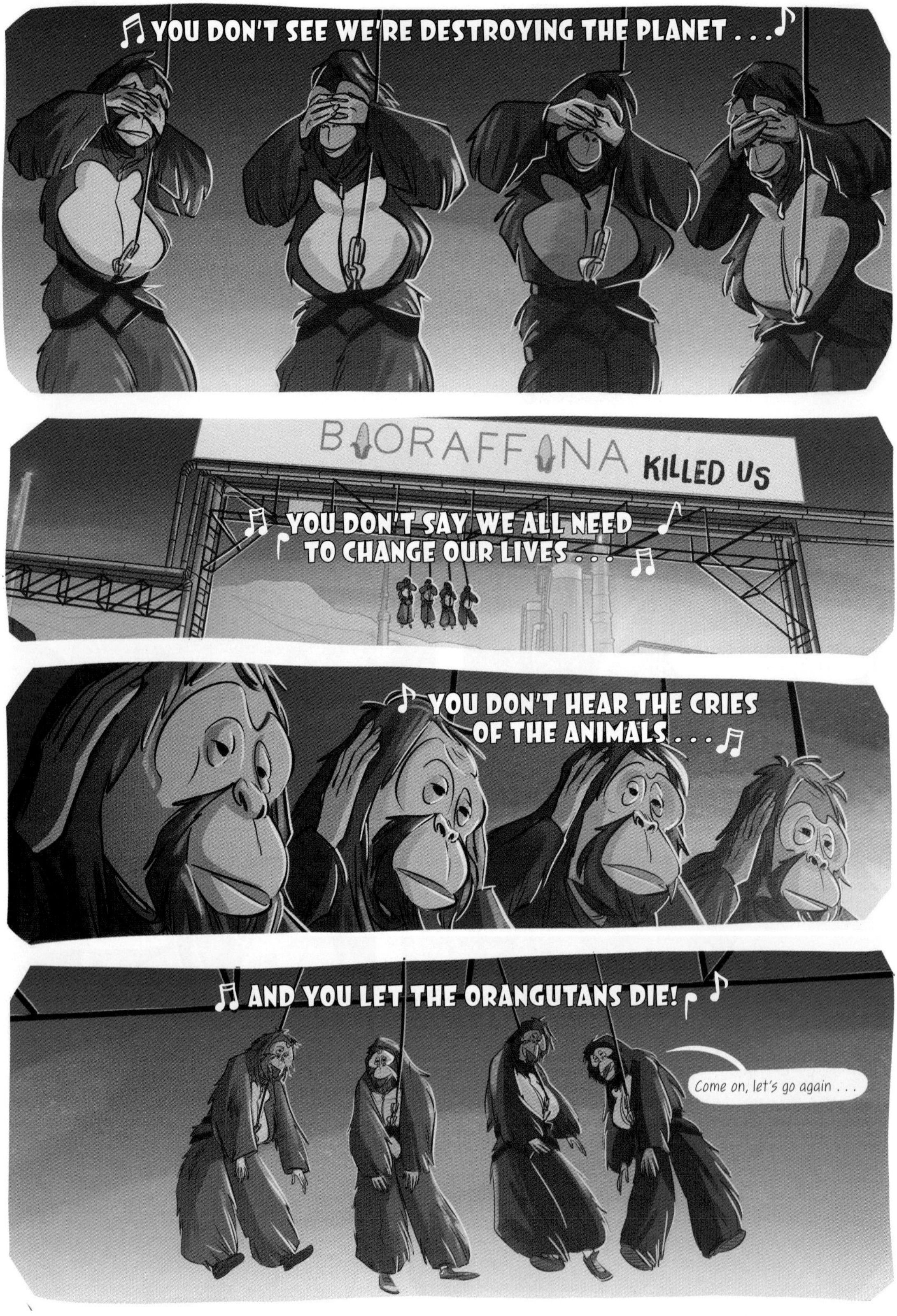
YOU DON'T SEE WE'RE DESTROYING THE PLANET . . .
BIORAFFINA KILLED US
YOU DON'T SAY WE ALL NEED TO CHANGE OUR LIVES . . .
YOU DON'T HEAR THE CRIES OF THE ANIMALS . . .
AND YOU LET THE ORANGUTANS DIE!
Come on, let's go again . . .

♪ YOU DON'T SEE . . . ♪

Get them down from there!

This instant!!!

OK, but, uh . . . how?

YOU DON'T SAY . . . ♪

And eject these journalists!!

We can't do anything, they're on a public road.

YOU DON'T HEAR . . . ♪ ♪

So what do we do!?!

Well, boss . . .

I guess we wait.

♪ AND YOU LET THE ORANGUTANS DIE! ♪

It really worked!

We've already got views on Insta.

And on TikTok too!

Two or three more times?

Gotta be sure we've got some good clips!

Here at the Bioraffina refinery, we're witnessing an unusual sight!

Ha ha! Bravo, Emma!

Here's your medication . . .

Look! *Emma's* on TV!

Not quite, Mom.

She's sleeping on the lawn with her . .

. . . you let the orangutans die!

That's Emma! On TV!

No! Not again!

She is in *so* much trouble . . .

Now, now, dear. You can scold her later.

But she wants to change the world. Nothing is braver than that.

So right now, be proud!

You're right, Mom.

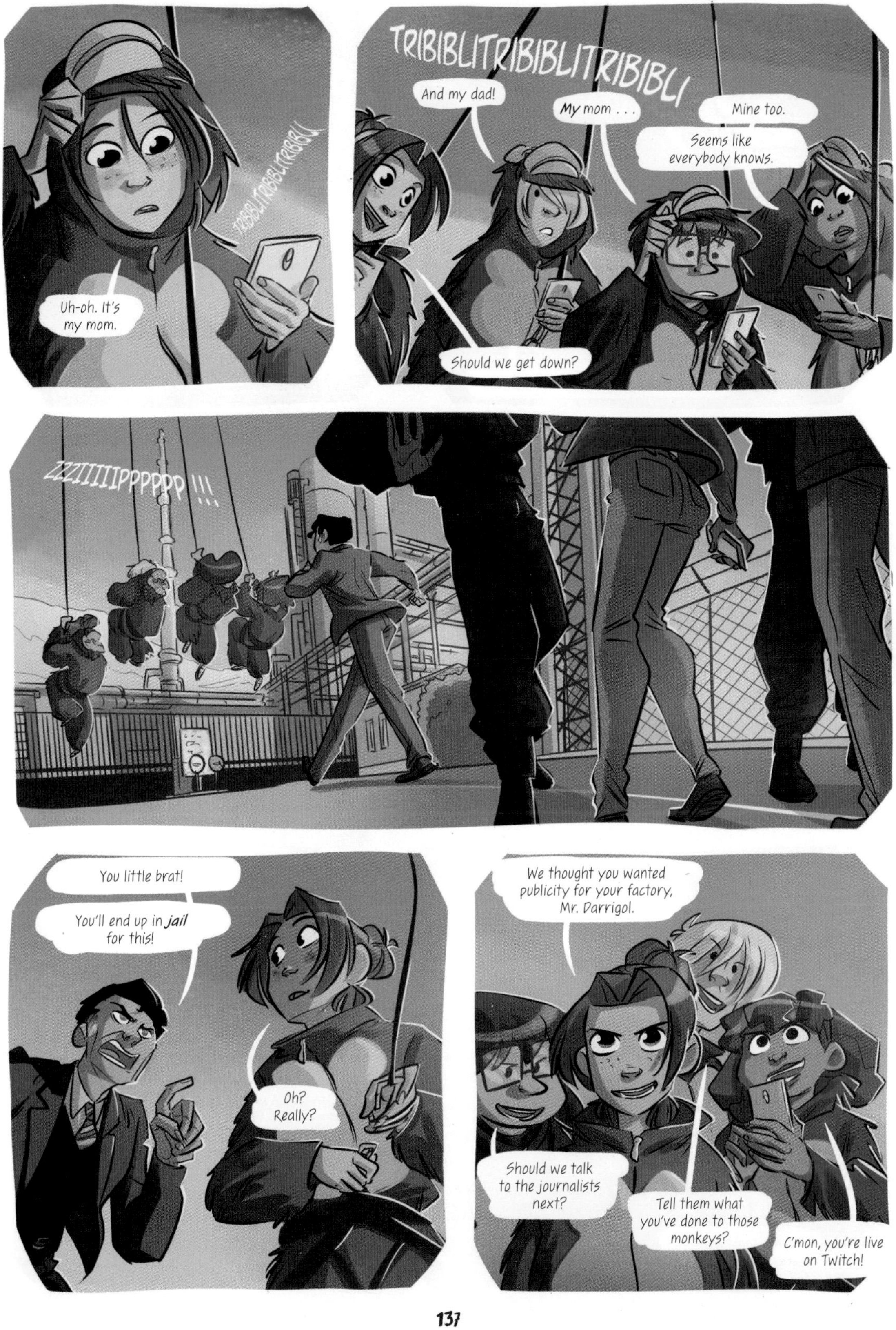
Uh-oh. It's my mom.
TRIBIBLITRIBIBLITRIBIBLI
TRIBIBLITRIBIBLITRIBIBLI
And my dad!
My mom . . .
Mine too.
Seems like everybody knows.
Should we get down?
ZZIIIIIPPPPPP !!!
You little brat!
You'll end up in *jail* for this!
Oh? Really?
We thought you wanted publicity for your factory, Mr. Darrigol.
Should we talk to the journalists next?
Tell them what you've done to those monkeys?
C'mon, you're live on Twitch!

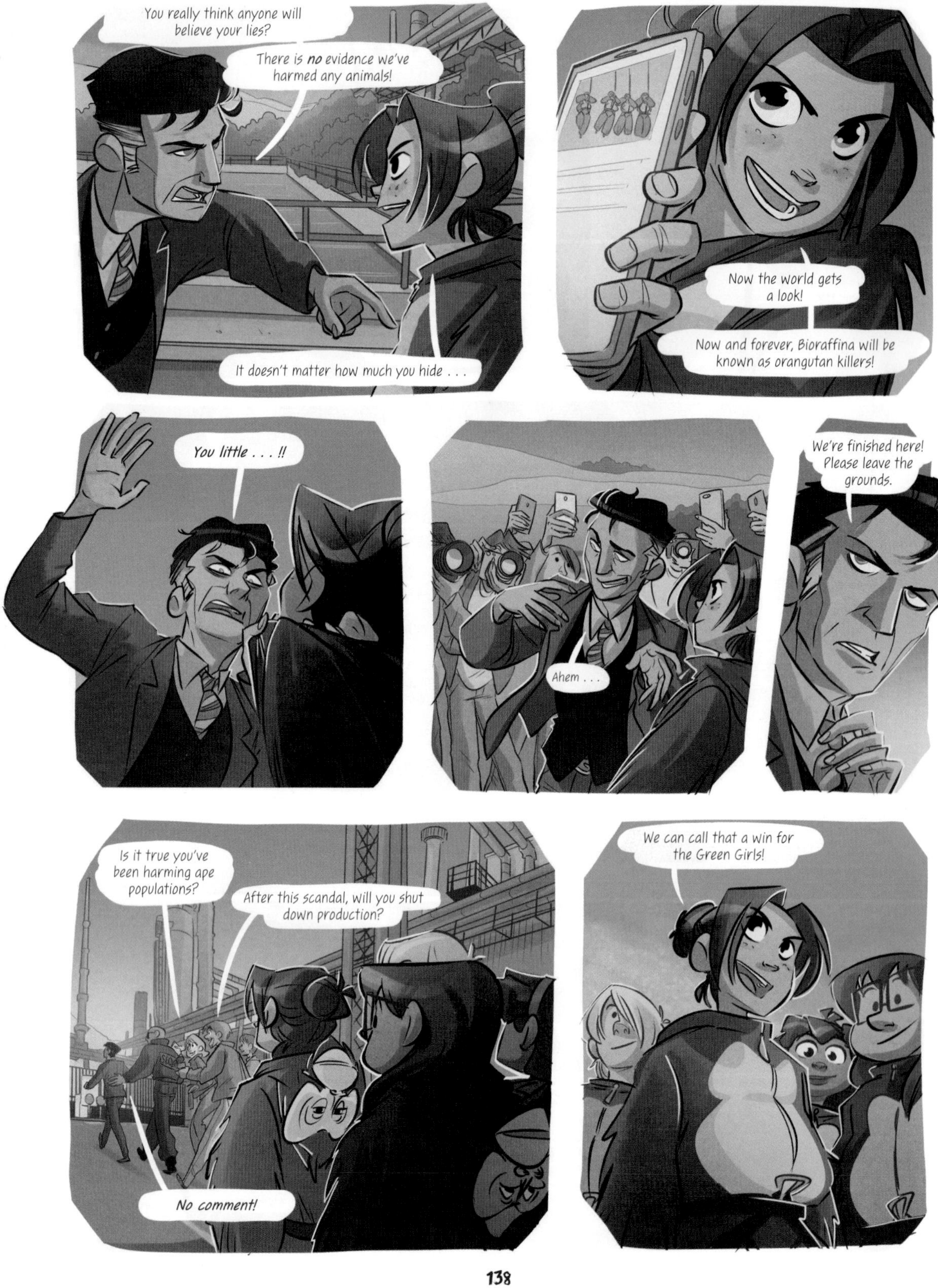
You really think anyone will believe your lies?
There is **no** evidence we've harmed any animals!
It doesn't matter how much you hide . . .
Now the world gets a look!
Now and forever, Bioraffina will be known as orangutan killers!
You little . . . !!
Ahem . . .
We're finished here! Please leave the grounds.
Is it true you've been harming ape populations?
After this scandal, will you shut down production?
No comment!
We can call that a win for the Green Girls!

On this side of the planet, no one sees the damage of deforestation . . .

But people need to know.

That's our mission in the Green Girls . . .

TRIBIBIBLITRIBLI

Hi . . . Dad? What's up?

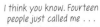

I think you know. Fourteen people just called me . . .

After seeing you on TV!

You'll never stop, will you?

Just as soon as people stop polluting.

But I'll have some days to spare first.

Gotta go. Mom's here.

You're my daughter, all right. Stubborn as a mule.

Take care!

Don't make that face, Mom!

We **had** to do something.

It's not that.

It's Manon. She . . .

Manon?

139

I have something for you.

The day before she passed, she said she wanted you to have it.

She got it from *her* grandmother.

That's her *brooch!*

Thank you, Grandma!

We'll all miss your Manon.

It's such a nice line she had engraved.

Simone Perry
1933 - 2022

The best is yet to come!

That's what she always said when things were at their worst.

CLIP

Will your family keep this house?

We're not sure.

My mom's waiting for my uncle in Australia to come back before deciding.

It'd be a shame to let it go.

The rose garden is beautiful!

It was her pride and joy.

She'd walk here on sunny days . . .

Hey, I wanted to tell you something . . .

Finally . . .

Yeah?

BEEEPP BEEEEEEEPP

Whoops, that's Piero! He's my ride back home . . .

Gotta jet. See you at school?

Sure, Silas . . .

I didn't think we'd see each other so soon, Ms. Delaney.

There's been a lot of talk about you!

I know, Judge.

But I don't understand what I'm doing here! I didn't **destroy** anything . . .

What Emma means to say is . . .

I know **exactly** what she means.

You're here because Mr. Darrigol has lodged a complaint concerning the defiling of private property and defamation.

Judge B

But that's all wrong!

He's the one **defiling** our **planet!**

Calm down, young lady.

Listen to me carefully. You're right . . .

You followed my guidelines. No vandalism. No destruction of property. So the complaint isn't valid. Technically.

And I advise you to make that known to as many people as possible. Why not on the Green Girls Instagram?

So I'm . . . free?

And I can tell the world Darrigol is a lying . . .

Careful, Emma.

And you still have two more days to spend at Clearer Rivers.

142

"After making a spectacle in front of members of the press . . ."

"And following outcry on social media . . ."

"The chief executive of Bioraffina, J.J. Darrigol, has resigned."

Yeaaah!!

That's **really** a win!

We might be viral stars . . .

Like I'm the **queen** of TikTok . . .

BLEGH!

But we didn't get out of garbage duty.

You know what?

I bet Manon's really proud of you up there.

Squeak!

Yes. I believe it too.

Hey Emma, with everything that happened . . .

I, uh, didn't have a chance to tell you . . .

Well, um, that . . .

I think I know.

SMACK!

143

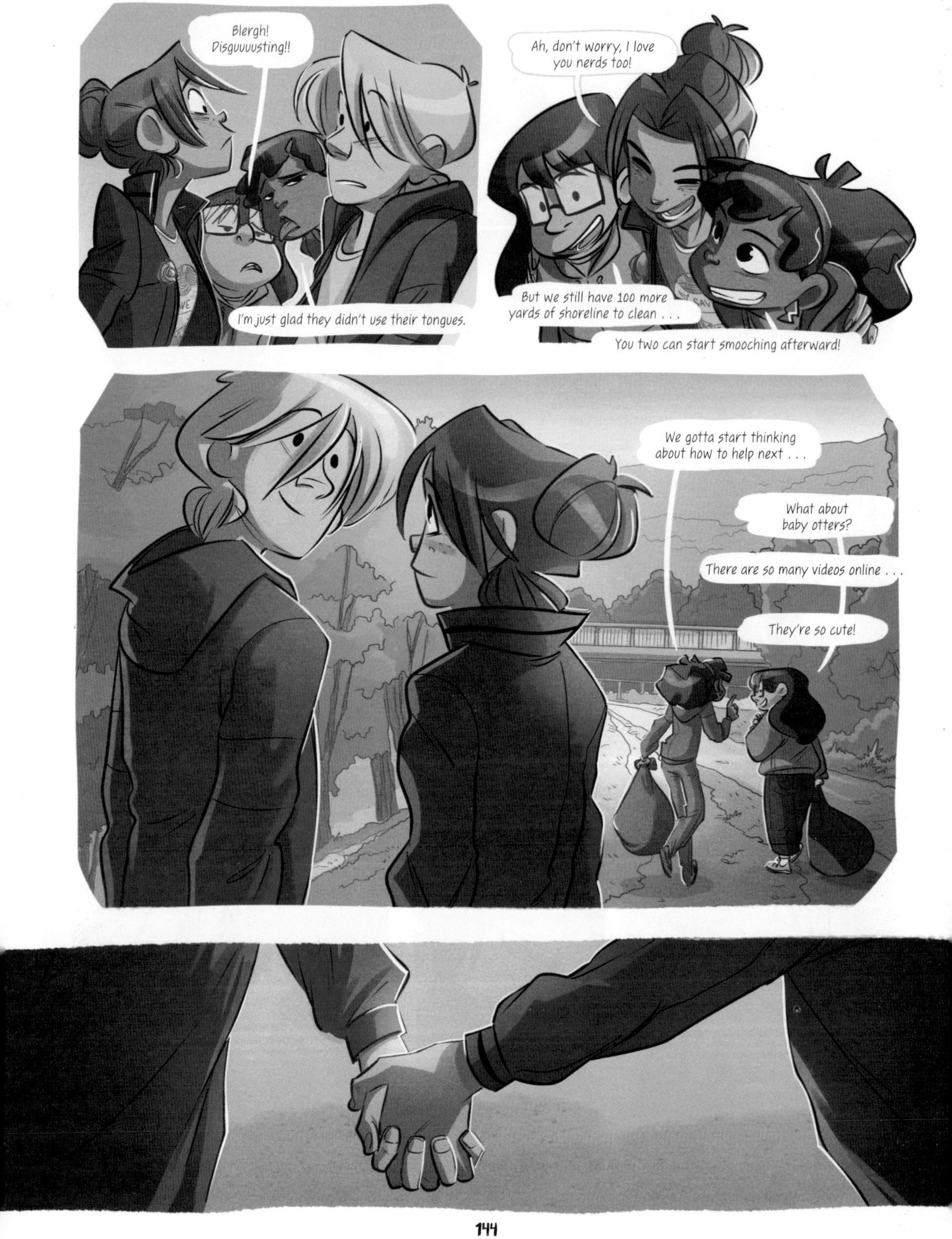
Blergh! Disguuuusting!!
I'm just glad they didn't use their tongues.
Ah, don't worry, I love you nerds too!
But we still have 100 more yards of shoreline to clean . . .
You two can start smooching afterward!
We gotta start thinking about how to help next . . .
What about baby otters?
There are so many videos online . . .
They're so cute!